SQUID SEASON

SQUID SEASON

Maithy Vu

Copyright © 2022 by Maithy Vu

First paperback edition November 2022

Text edited by Aubrie Goslin and Cleo Miele

Cover design by Zakarias Fariury

Author photograph by Maria Oglesby

ISBN 978-0-9963822-0-5 (paperback)
ISBN 978-0-9963822-1-2 (eBook)

www.maithyvu.com

To the young—

Sew your dreams within your sails,

raise your anchors, and weather the storm

Prologue

T he squid was sought by all and spoken of by none. They pretended not to want it, as though wanting it were shameful. It was said to live in the depths of the purple waters so far from shore, only the most determined had ever ventured to find it. Some claimed to have found it, yet none could describe what it looked like. This didn't stop others from seeking it, however, because those who found it always came back different.

Our story begins in the middle of the sea, where the sky is painted yellow and orange, blue and pink. It is neither now nor then. There is endless time, yet none at all. Days are marked only by the strength of the sun.

A faint clinking sound can be heard upon a ship that sits on still water. The ship's beams, made of wooden trunks, are accompanied by sails made of foliage. Vines embellish the vessel instead of rope, and its hull is made of earth. If one were not looking carefully, they might mistake the ship for a small island.

Below the deck, four cots are arranged in a circle: one made of spontaneity and regret, one full of tosses and turns, one of cold and distrust, and one of frenzy and birth.

In the adjoining kitchen, a table sits in the center. It is there that the clinking sound originates, in the midst of a small dinner party.

There are four present. How or when they got there, we may never know. What we do know is that they are four very different people seeking one thing for four very different reasons.

SOLOMAN.
I'm curious as to why we're all here, I admit.

WINNIE.
We're not obligated to speak of it.

AUGUST.
It's true. We have a right to our secrecy.
One should have the decency—

SOLOMAN.
I didn't ask. I merely stated I'm curious.

CAMELLE.
You see, he wasn't serious.
Now, may we enjoy our supper?

SOLOMAN.
Cheers. Pass the butter.

CAMELLE.
Does anyone want my bread?

WINNIE.
This butter doesn't spread . . .

SOLOMAN.
Pass it anyway. Now, I have a hunch
that we make a fairly good bunch.
Since we're all here together,
let us get to know one another.
Not to worry, I'll begin.
People call me Soloman.

The butter melted onto Soloman's bread. He held
the slice between his teeth as he poured a bottle of red into
his glass.

CAMELLE.
My name's Camelle.
I hope you're all well!

AUGUST.
Right, then, if we must . . .
Evening. I'm August.

They all looked to Winnie, who was poking at her
bread with a knife. She stopped suddenly.

WINNIE.
My name is none of your concern.

SOLOMAN.
Looks like that one we'll have to earn.

CAMELLE.
Oh, I'd love to learn who you all are!
In your opinion, what's most important by far?

AUGUST.
In all my tangled life,
my blood is where my duty lies.
I walk with this rule, and I
am hardly dissatisfied.

CAMELLE.
What is your family like?
Have you any children or wife?

AUGUST.
Not yet, but soon, I intend.
For now, my folks are where my time is spent.

He sliced his bread in half, buttered one half but not
the other, and then stared at his plate.

CAMELLE.
Captain, what gives you bliss?

SOLOMAN.
A woman's kiss,
though I am not yet captain of the sea.

CAMELLE.
You are and always will be captain to me.

She held out her bread. Soloman gently took it.
The other two looked at one another and shrugged.

SOLOMAN.
What gives you bliss, my jewel?

CAMELLE.
Simply abiding by one rule:
be good to all, and to all, give comfort.
Always soothe the pain of others—

Winnie spat out her drink with a scoff.

WINNIE.
In your bubble, you may be a queen,
but there are things you haven't yet seen.

All eyes were on Camelle as she gathered herself.

CAMELLE.
I suppose, but I am trying.
Though, would you mind specifying?

WINNIE.
The dark and the cold of man
who'll take from you all he can.
His nature is hungry and cruel.
One must not act a fool.

Soloman broke the silence with laughter.

SOLOMAN.
You are quite the character, my girl,
one as rare as a lustrous pearl.

WINNIE.
I am not a girl, nor am I yours.
As for pearls, I find them a bore.
I'm more of an iron woman myself.

SOLOMAN.
Ah, then I confuse you with someone else.

He raised a crimson glass.

SOLOMAN.
Let us toast to a wondrous trek!

CAMELLE.
Hush! A noise upon the deck!

The ship faltered and became directionless. A loud
boom followed, and each diner gasped.

AUGUST.
Shall we see what's going on?

SOLOMAN.
The captain must have had a yawn.
I wouldn't worry—

CAMELLE.
Another noise! Hurry!

The four scurried up the stairs as another blast nearly split their ears. They raced toward the middle of the deck, only to discover the ominous emptiness of an abandoned wheel at the helm.

SOLOMAN.
Where the blazes can he be?

AUGUST.
He must have been taken by the sea.

SOLOMAN.
Taken by th—
Do you mean he fell?
Wouldn't we have heard him yell?

WINNIE.
The noise we heard was not a splash.

CAMELLE.
Agreed. It was more of a crash!

AUGUST.
Four crashes, to be exact.
Though I'd say we couldn't have been attacked.

SOLOMAN.
Does anyone have a suggestion?

WINNIE.
No, but I do have a question.
Did anyone actually see a captain?

CAMELLE.
We were all quite distracted . . .
but of course there was!

SOLOMAN.
Wait. She has a fair point, because—

AUGUST.
I saw him. He was in white.

CAMELLE.
Oh no, that isn't right.
She was most definitely in green.

AUGUST.
Sh—
Are you certain you've seen—?

SOLOMAN.
Were they wearing a hat?

CAMELLE.
I don't recall that.

AUGUST.
Neither do I.

SOLOMAN.
What color were their eyes?

AUGUST.
Well how are we supposed to know?
We weren't eyeing him from head to toe!

SOLOMAN.
Then how are we to take your word?

AUGUST.
If there was no captain, what were the noises heard?

No one had an answer.

CAMELLE.
Well, what are we to do now?
We have to get there, but how?

AUGUST.
Didn't Soloman mention he could sail?
Surely, you'll steer us now without fail?

They all looked desperately at Soloman.

SOLOMAN.
Uh . . . I . . . of course I would.

WINNIE.
Good.

AUGUST.
Shall we bring our supper up here?

SOLOMAN.
Yes, I could use a drink while I steer.

Soloman took the wheel.

Part I:
Soloman

S oloman had a way of making everybody feel special yet insignificant at the same time. He could say things that hit right in the heart, and then leave one wondering if he said the same things to everybody. It wasn't intentional; it was a result of how he felt about himself. Soloman thought he could only be one of two things: the greatest to ever live, or the one everyone wanted gone.

Ever since he was young, Soloman had wanted to be a ship's captain. It was not until our fated dinner party, however, that he had ever sailed a ship. Though, this fact never stopped him from spreading the word that he had, for it made him quite popular with the opposite sex.

Soloman was summer. Women never had a problem shedding their clothes for him, while men loved to converse with him over drinks. Around him, they were carefree and spontaneous. The past and the future never mattered. Life was a series of moments where the consequences were of no concern. Yet, due to his nature, most would eventually regret their time with him.

* * *

SOLOMAN.
I thought I had commanded
that you don't return empty-handed.

AUGUST.
You're not in your right mind if you think
I'd actually let you steer and drink.

August was one of the few people Soloman
interacted with who seemed to have a problem with him.
Unsure as to why that was, Soloman simply deemed it
jealousy.

SOLOMAN.
Ah, aren't you a responsible one?
I can't say you're any fun.

Despite the disapproval Soloman sensed from
August, there was something about him that he found quite
comforting.

SOLOMAN.
Well, if you brought nothing to pour,
then what exactly are you here for?

AUGUST.
Thought you might need assistance.
In case you get . . . tired, for instance.

SOLOMAN.
You act as though you're older.
I don't need watching over.

AUGUST.
Right. I have better things to do
than to stay and argue with you.
I'll leave you alone, then, but don't doze off.
The last thing we need is to get lost.

Winnie wandered up the deck with a book in her hand and a bread roll in her mouth. Camelle followed close behind, weaving through the trees that covered the vessel.

CAMELLE.
You think you know all and more
when you've never seen the sea before.
Now here I stand, so small and trite
against this vast, enthralling sight.
Though it makes me feel unaware,
I can't wait to breathe the things out there!

Soloman couldn't help but notice the annoyed look on Winnie's face. Before he could interject, August turned to Camelle.

AUGUST.
Miss . . .? I'm sorry, I've forgotten your name.

CAMELLE.
Oh, don't be ashamed.
It's Camelle. Did you need something?

AUGUST.
Well, I was just thinking . . .
Soloman might need a little company,
and it seemed you two got along quite easily.

CAMELLE.
Oh . . . of course. Will do.

AUGUST.
Thank you.

August made his way over to Winnie, who was sitting upon the earth of the ship's hull, leaning against a tree trunk. Although they provided only whispers, Soloman could hear snippets of their conversation.

AUGUST.
Would it be all right if I joined you, miss?
I said it earlier, but again, I'm August.

Winnie took the bread roll from her mouth.

WINNIE.
Do you also find her excruciating?

AUGUST.
She's not *that* aggravating.

WINNIE.
No one should radiate that much joy.
That amount of fervor is always a ploy.

August let out a soft chuckle and sat beside her. Soloman looked nervously at Camelle, but she didn't seem to have heard the comment. She had stopped about ten steps from him, avoiding his eyes. Little did Soloman know, this was the closest Camelle could place herself to him without losing her ability to speak.

CAMELLE.
I never thought I'd see you again.

SOLOMAN.
You look just like you did then.

Camelle met his stare, and Soloman gave a silent apology he hoped she understood.

*   *   *

"Children? Get back here this instant!"

*"Soloman, that's Ms. Vincent!
If she finds us, she'll botch our ears!"*

*"She'll never find us here.
Quit worrying about everything."*

"What if she gives our parents a ring?"

*"We'll deal with it when the time comes.
Now, let me see your tongue.
Ah, yes, the color of lime.
And what of mine?"*

"It's red!"

"Red, you said?
Red like a tongue or red like a cherry?"

"Red like a berry!"

"Success!
Shall we save the rest?
When I'm a captain, we'll buy all the sweets we crave."

"And what shall I do when you're fighting the waves?"

"You'll be here in our house made of cake!"

"What? You mean stay here lying awake,
just waiting for you to come back?"

"I wouldn't put it like that.
Come on, don't start a fuss.
Remember the poem read to us?
'From shore to sea
and sea to shore
you are mine
and I am yours.
Mi amor.'"

"'Mi amor.'"

"This is your last call, children!"

"Let's go, Elle, before she counts to ten.

We'll tell her you fell and hurt your knee."

"Like she'll ever believe that story."

* * *

CAMELLE.
What are you doing here, anyway?

SOLOMAN.
I should ask you the same.

CAMELLE.
I don't have to tell you a thing.

SOLOMAN.
All right, cheers. I deserved that sting.
I suppose you're standing here in place
so you can finally sock me in the face.

CAMELLE.
I was asked to keep you company.

SOLOMAN.
Ah. That man seems to distrust me.

They turned toward August, who was shifting
uncomfortably on the floor while conversing with Winnie.
Every so often, he would adjust his sweater vest or brush dirt
off his shoes.

CAMELLE.
Perhaps you gave him reason.

SOLOMAN.
Something you have expertise in.
Tell me, what crime have I done?

CAMELLE.
Your attire, for one.

Soloman looked down at his exposed arms, knees, and feet.

SOLOMAN.
Well, I normally go without.

CAMELLE.
Is that really what we're talking about?
After all this time—a joke is what you have to say?
I should have known it'd go this way.
You're incapable of anything else.

She began to leave, but then . . .

SOLOMAN.
Camelle.

She turned back around. In an instant, it became impossible for either of them to look away. Soloman noticed the water rising from Camelle's eyes like the ocean's unforgiving tide. A thousand unspoken words drowned them both. He opened his mouth to speak, only to be interrupted by a faint tune growing louder with every second.

August and Winnie approached. Upon their arrival, Camelle quickly wiped her cheeks with her palms.

AUGUST.
Do you hear it as well?

SOLOMAN.
We all do, as far as I can tell.

The four looked up to find the music resonating from a thousand beetles adrift in the sky. Their wings beat rapidly beneath shells of metallic green. It was an emerald symphony—a gathering of musicians as identical as soldiers, yet, if one listened intently, one would notice they were playing different parts.

Soloman let go of the wheel and pulled Camelle to him.

SOLOMAN.
Come, my jewel. Dance to the beat!
Goodness, Elle. Move your feet!

CAMELLE.
Don't you have to steer?

SOLOMAN.
Look around! The water's clear!

He moved her about the ship into a playful waltz as the beetles swirled overhead. Her dress bloomed as she spun, swaying with the sound. The sun bounced off the beetles' shells, nearly blinding them with their seductive glow.

* * *

When they were children, Soloman and Camelle would dance around her mother's living room. Camelle's residence was a pastel paradise adorned with faux-fur rugs, chandeliers, and porcelain vases.

Camelle's mother also looked fit to appear in a magazine spread. She would wear form-fitting skirts and oxford pumps even while at home. While they danced, she'd have a smoke on the balcony or play the piano along with the record player. She made Soloman wash his hands often, and never allowed him on the couch. Sometimes, she would ask about his father then scoff at whatever answer she received.

Soloman's father was a fisherman. He set out to sea during the night and slept throughout the day. As soon as Soloman came home from school, his father would get up, which gave them a few hours to spend together in the afternoon. The two lived in a small stone cottage just beside the docks.

On certain days, Camelle would swing by, and the children would finish their studies while Soloman's father whipped up their favorite: cod and chips with a scoop of slaw. At times, he would place a carrot against his hand and pretend to chop his finger off. The children would scream and laugh until their bellies ached.

It was moments like these from his childhood when Soloman wanted to be like his father.

* * *

SOLOMAN.
You two! Don't be a stick-in-the-mud!
Grab the other and dance with us!

A blur, which Soloman could only assume was
Winnie, shouted back.

WINNIE.
I don't dance!

The beetles stopped in mid-air as though a record
had scratched. They hovered for a moment, casting a
massive dark shadow over the ship, then zoomed toward the
sun in silence, the wispy green cloud disappearing from
sight.
Soloman turned to August.

SOLOMAN.
Sorry, mate, you missed your chance.

Soloman's light dimmed as Camelle pulled away. He
mustered nearly all of his remaining energy to not look at
her as he headed back toward the wheel.

SOLOMAN.
Now, I don't mean to fuss,
but we've got a long journey ahead of us.
Quit giving me your useless stares
and grab us a bottle from downstairs!

* * *

Soloman had decided he wanted to be a ship's captain when his father tried to take him to a restaurant for his tenth birthday. When they walked through the door, it was the fanciest place Soloman had ever seen. People chatted through the clinking of golden silverware and wine glasses. Tables were lit by flickering candles and chandeliers dangling from a high ceiling.

"Just this once," his father said, squeezing his hand. *" We'll dine like kings."*

When the host greeted them, Soloman noticed he wrinkled his nose. Though Soloman's father had worn his best coat, his hands and shoes still revealed his life as a fisherman.

The host informed them that the restaurant was much too crowded to seat anybody at the moment. Soloman's father insisted they had a reservation, but the host simply smiled and suggested the diner across the street.

Then a man in a white uniform walked through the door. The host straightened his back before bowing his head in deference. The man asked for a table by a window, insisted no customers be seated around him, and requested for bouillabaisse to be brought over immediately.

"Of course, Captain," the host replied. *"Right this way."*

When the servers saw that uniform, they parted the seas for the man. No one questioned him or told him he didn't belong. They just gave him what he wanted, even when what he wanted was unreasonable.

And it was through this moment that Soloman decided he needed to be more than his father. Nothing mattered if you didn't have a title, for it was titles that made people listen, titles that proved your worth, and titles that made you visible.

* * *

SOLOMAN.
Darling, lean any further
and you'll topple over.
Let's not give us a fright.

Soloman steadied the wheel with one hand and a drink with the other. Camelle stood on her toes at the starboard, gazing beyond the line of the sea. She clutched the edge, warm air welcoming her face, as the sky faded from a burning orange to twilight.

AUGUST.
Hard to believe it, but he's right.
It's best to stay away from the edge.
Besides, it's time we get some rest.

Winnie, who'd had her nose buried in the same page for twenty minutes, snapped her book shut. She sprinted to the port and, to everyone's surprise, vomited into the sea.

SOLOMAN.
Ha! Isn't that just splendid?
For some, the edge is recommended!

August offered Winnie his handkerchief.

AUGUST.
Just a bit of seasickness.
It happens to the best of us.

SOLOMAN.
I know I hurl at least twice a season.
Though with me, it's for different reasons.

He raised his glass before finishing it with one gulp.
Winnie wiped August's handkerchief across her
mouth.

WINNIE.
I assume you don't want me to return this.

AUGUST.
I strongly encourage you to keep it.

Camelle picked up Winnie's book and handed it to
her.

CAMELLE.
Perhaps a cool soak is what you need.
It'll make you feel better in this heat.

WINNIE.
Considering I can no longer see the page,
I don't suppose there's any reason to stay.

While Winnie was still full of snark, she also seemed
a bit absent. As she passed Soloman, he noticed she had that
smell that emanated whenever someone came in from the

cold outside. It was neither welcome nor unwelcome—just a presence that hovered before it was forgotten.

Winnie got to the stairwell when August caught up to her. He pulled a silk satchel from the pocket of his trousers.

AUGUST.
Here, you'll want to smell these.
Nausea can be eased by mint leaves.

Winnie took the satchel and stared at it in her hand.

WINNIE.
You carry these around in your pants?

AUGUST.
I . . . I like the smell of them.

Winnie disappeared below deck as quickly as she had vomited.

Laughter came from the wheel.

SOLOMAN.
Was that a romantic attempt?

CAMELLE.
Soloman, would it hurt to show some respect?

August slipped his hands into his pockets and shuffled toward them.

AUGUST.
I won't satisfy you with a response.

Anyway, I think I spotted a yawn.
Perhaps you should let me steer.

SOLOMAN.
No, thanks. I've got it from here.
The yawn was due to boredom
from being 'round your decorum.

AUGUST.
There's no need to act tall.
You haven't rested at all.

SOLOMAN.
No rest for the wicked, lad.

AUGUST.
I can't argue with that.
Camelle, I trust you'll keep him awake.

SOLOMAN.
Been doing so since our first days.

Soloman expected curiosity from August after that statement. He was surprised when August retreated without another word.

CAMELLE.
Why must you tease the man?

SOLOMAN.
Because I can.

CAMELLE.
He seems so sad to me.
Like he needs to be set free.
Perhaps we can bring him some fun.

SOLOMAN.
There's no need to analyze everyone.

CAMELLE.
Ironic coming from the man
most difficult to understand.
Are you sure you don't need to rest?

SOLOMAN.
Darling, sailing is what I know best.

* * *

To Soloman, life was merely brief encounters with the sun. It was random in its appearances, though all to be enjoyed. That was the beauty of it. He preferred it that way. As long as things didn't matter, he was free. Perhaps that was why Soloman never spent much time anywhere. The more time spent on something, the more it would begin to matter. And the more something began to matter, the more there was room for disappointment.

As a result, Soloman was used to interactions feeling forced. When he spoke to others, it was a series of steps he followed, a conscious process he'd memorized. It was the only way that he could keep things from mattering. He felt awful about it, for he knew it wasn't mechanical to them—that it was very real in their eyes—and he tried hard to give others the most thrilling experience they could have with someone like him.

Yet, with Camelle, there was never a process. He found himself thrown off, flustered between the blissful moments. This unraveled him, for with others, he didn't mind that it was all fabricated and meant nothing. But if he went on to spend more time with Camelle, only to discover it was not what he believed, well that . . . that would destroy him indefinitely.

* * *

CAMELLE.
You set sail a lot, I bet.

SOLOMAN.
Indeed, any chance I can get.

The stillness of Camelle's emotions rippled the pool of Soloman's.

SOLOMAN.
Go on, do it. Sock me in the nose.
All this time and you've stayed composed.
Now there's no sight of the other two,
so go, do what you've been wanting to do.

CAMELLE.
It's been six years and you're still the same.
Just as cheeky, just as vain.
You assume you left a wound that deep?

SOLOMAN.
Just hit me so I can sleep.

CAMELLE.
I was asked to keep you awake.

SOLOMAN.
You're beautiful, by the way.
Always have been.

Perhaps it was the extra drink, or the sky growing darker that gave him that bit of courage.

CAMELLE.
Good night, Soloman.

*   *   *

It wasn't until they were teenagers that things began to grow difficult with Camelle. It had been easy for Soloman to be by Camelle's side as children, but young adults weren't quite as accepting. The boys would press him for answers, and the girls he went after always hesitated. It soon became clear to Soloman that they needed to spend more time apart.

He did his best to ease her into it. First, he turned down her invitation to come over for dinner and said he had to complete a project with a few classmates. That much was true. The week after, he let her know he was going to the cinema with a girl from his class. That was also true. Then he told her that his father was taking him fishing. That was not true.

Each time he turned her down, Soloman was
surprised to find that Camelle never questioned him, never
acted disappointed. And the few days a month that he did
spend with her were just as they had always been.

* * *

As the days passed, the leafy sails grew apricots and
peaches and cherries. They all retreated to their beds in the
night except for Soloman, who would remain behind the
wheel. He could go many moons without sleeping. Little did
he know, the others were just the same.

Soloman had tried his best to ensure that everyone
had a good time during their days, offering humor and
plenty of refills of drinks. It seemed Camelle had forgotten
all that had pained her, and as Soloman locked eyes with her
now and then, they almost became children again.

One morning, just as dawn greeted Soloman, so did
the presence of Camelle wandering up the deck.

SOLOMAN.
Morning, Elle.
Sleep well?

CAMELLE.
Ah, that face.
Enough to make a girl faint.

For a moment, Soloman forgot where they were and
how old they'd gotten. For a moment, he remembered who
he was and not who he had become.

Camelle made her way to the edge of the ship, staring at the horizon revealing itself to them. She grabbed hold of a vine and hoisted herself up onto the edge. Before Soloman could say a word, she let go and plummeted into the sea.

Soloman abandoned the wheel and raced over to the edge, his heart thumping faster than his steps. Below, Camelle floated on her back as gracefully as a water lily.

CAMELLE.
Oh, so you *do* care!

SOLOMAN.
You're very irritating, I hope you're aware.

Camelle continued to float, heading toward a small island. As he watched her, Soloman heard footsteps behind him.

AUGUST.
The mornings have gotten hotter.
. . . Is that Camelle in the water?

SOLOMAN.
Yes. It seems she's found land.

WINNIE.
Huh. I'll be damned.

AUGUST.
Look at those rocks on the island.
Don't they look like—

WINNIE.
Lions.

SOLOMAN.
Anyone for a swim?

AUGUST.
We're not jumping in.
We need to stay on path.

SOLOMAN.
Someone's going to have to get her back.

Soloman pulled his shirt over his head and jumped. His body crashed beneath the surface, clearing his mind before air greeted him once more. He glided through the water like he was born in it, arms resting against his sides like fins.

AUGUST.
For goodness' sake.

WINNIE.
To hell with it. I've made worse mistakes.

Winnie tossed a vine over the edge and slowly descended into the water. When she reached the end of her rope, she let herself fall onto her back.
A splash followed her seconds later.

SOLOMAN.
Now, is that some sort of lopsided fish,

or am I really seeing our friend August?

Behind Winnie, August flailed his arms, sputtering water out of his mouth.

AUGUST.
I struggle with things I find unsanitary,
though I appreciate the commentary.

CAMELLE.
Oh, you're all joining me!

AUGUST.
Right. Not exactly.
You're slowing down the rest of us.

SOLOMAN.
Come now, what's the rush?

And so they glowed, illuminated by the water's warm embrace.

* * *

Memories were always peculiar to Soloman. There were some in which he could only remember what was said, and some wherein he could only remember what was seen. Others combined sight and smell, sound and touch. If he was lucky, or perhaps very unlucky, he could grasp multiple senses of certain memories. Those were the ones that never escaped.

Once in a while, Soloman found himself trying to put together the pieces, hoping whatever fragments he collected would give meaning to his life. Perhaps the music he had once heard would harmonize with what he could be. Perhaps the moments he held onto would revolve around his fate like it was the sun. Without his memories, he would float through time with no order at all, like a dandelion seed drifting in the wind.

Soloman dreaded these moments of weakness. Whenever they happened, he simply shook his head and finished his drink.

* * *

AUGUST.
How much time has passed?

They floated on their backs, staring up at a sapphire sky for so long, they could not remember the clouds.

SOLOMAN.
Beats me. Why do you ask?

CAMELLE.
How much time? . . . I don't know.
Everything feels so . . . slow.

AUGUST.
What happened to the island?

CAMELLE.
It got too difficult to find it.

WINNIE.
I can't tell whether it's been minutes or days.
It's like trying to see through a haze.
Have I done too much,
or not enough?

AUGUST.
Perhaps we should head back now.

SOLOMAN.
Did you let the anchor down?

They glanced at the abandoned ship. All four swam
frantically until they realized there was hardly a breeze. One
by one, they climbed the hanging vine, their missions drifting
back to them with every stretch.

As Soloman swung his legs over the edge, he toppled
into Camelle. He held onto her shoulders to keep them
both steady, and it was only then that he noticed the lines
that had formed on her forehead over the years, the freckles
scattered across her cheeks, the crinkles on the sides of her
mouth. She looked at him just as intently. Comfort and
nervousness warred inside him.

CAMELLE.
Since you disappeared,
I always feared
our fate was at its end.
Now that you're here,
I realize what I should have feared
was seeing you again.

Soloman understood, though he did not say so.

AUGUST.
Pardon? You two knew each other in the past?

WINNIE.
Obviously. You couldn't cut the tension with an axe.

Soloman tore himself from Camelle. She composed herself, then picked up August's scarf on the floor, soaked from their thoughtlessness. She noticed the hand-sewn label.

CAMELLE.
Norwood?

SOLOMAN.
Oh, this will be good.

CAMELLE.
As in Norwood Matches?
Why, that's fantastic!

August cleared his throat.

AUGUST.
It's much more my father's business.
I'm merely an assistant . . .

CAMELLE.
Why, you're practically famous!

SOLOMAN.
Yes, think of all the candles lit.

CAMELLE.
Ignore him, August. I think it's great.

She handed the scarf back to him. August wrapped it twice around his neck.

WINNIE.
It's getting late.
Soloman, back behind the wheel.
I'll go and fix us a meal.

SOLOMAN.
Who knew the ice queen could fix a plate?

WINNIE.
Call her that again, and she'll poison your steak.

* * *

"Come on, Elle. It's my last night!"

"You know I'm afraid of heights!"

"Take my hand and quit moving so slow!"

"Are those rocks below?
It's late. I should be home."

"Just one more thing and then we'll go."

"My mother will wonder. You know this."

*"It won't hurt her to wait another minute.
It's only a few more steps to go.
Aaaand . . . behold!"*

*"Soloman, you always— Oh!
It's so beautiful!"*

"Elle . . . I'll be gone a long time."

"I know, but we'll write."

"I just don't know what'll happen."

"What'll happen is you'll be a captain."

* * *

The laughter that echoed from the ship was almost unrecognizable. The four had somehow forgotten the troubles of their pasts and began to grow an unexpected fondness for each other.

On this night, they had set down blankets and gathered by the wheel so Soloman could chime in on the fun. Every now and then, Winnie would toss a grape his way, which Soloman would catch with his mouth.

August threw down a handful of cards.

AUGUST.
How I managed to lose that round is beyond me.

SOLOMAN.
Ah, that's because Camelle's full of trickery.

Camelle scooped a pile of coins toward herself.

AUGUST.
Much stealth from someone so small!

WINNIE.
Perhaps I do like her after all.

AUGUST.
What about you, Soloman?
Would you like to buy in?

SOLOMAN.
No, thank you. I don't make bets.
The last thing I need is even more debt.

AUGUST.
Right. It's just a few coins.
It doesn't take that much to join.
What's the matter? Afraid you'll lose?
Or would you rather spend it on booze?

WINNIE.
Unless you two are married,
then this bickering is unnecessary.
Do we need to get you both a room,
or is it safe to say we can resume?

SOLOMAN.
Don't bring me into this.
He's the one who started it.

CAMELLE.
You two are like children sometimes.

SOLOMAN.
Is being economical such a crime?

* * *

When Soloman was four years old, his mother bought herself a new swimsuit in the dead of winter. It was yellow, with a bow across the chest and braided rope around the waist. She kept it tucked neatly in her drawer, waiting for the weather to warm so she could walk down to the beach. She couldn't wait to wear it—it was the best thing she'd ever owned, she claimed.

At the time, Soloman had developed a passion for physical comedy. He was wont to put on a pair of his father's trousers, smudge charcoal above his lip, and shuffle around holding an umbrella. However, the thing he wanted most was a top hat. He begged his folks for one, and when they hesitated, he explained how he'd be able to do a veritable wealth of tricks with it, like flip it onto his head, twirl it through his fingers, or perform magic.

His father tried to talk him out of it, but his mother stroked Soloman's hair and told him she would see what she could do.

Months later, on his birthday, Soloman woke to find a shiny black top hat sitting in the center of the kitchen table.

He threw his arms around his mother's neck as his father shook his head with a sigh.

Soloman immediately tossed the hat into the air, caught it with his head, and waddled around the kitchen. His mother clapped her hands in amusement.

"My little sunshine," she said. *"What would I do without you making me laugh?"*

Later that day, they were thrilled to discover the weather warm enough to visit the beach. Soloman stuck his head out the window, beamed at the cloudless sky, and made the announcement. His father packed a basket with bread and strawberry jam while his mother changed her clothes.

When she came to fetch Soloman from his room, however, he noticed she was wearing her old, worn white swimsuit. When he asked why she didn't have on the yellow one, she smiled and said she didn't like it as much as she'd thought.

Soloman was confused. She had waited all winter to wear it.

"The fabric itched," his mother continued. *"Now, put on your trunks and take your hat."*

*   *   *

AUGUST.
Nothing wrong with being economical.
I was referring to the empty bottles.
Don't you think you've had enough?

SOLOMAN.
Perhaps you need to lighten up.

You're the stuffiest man I've ever seen.
Look around you! We're at sea!
Wouldn't you like to feel bliss?
Here, take a swig of this.

CAMELLE.
August, don't mind his taunt.
Don't do it if you don't want—

AUGUST.
Pass it over here.

SOLOMAN.
Wh—? Let me clean my ears.
Did you say what I think—

AUGUST.
Pass the drink!

Soloman stuffed a cork into a near-empty glass and tossed it. It flew toward August's face before Winnie caught it mere inches from his nose.

Camelle turned to Soloman and muttered under her breath.

CAMELLE.
This is not what I meant.

Winnie yanked the cork from the bottle and handed it to August.

WINNIE.
To the present.

August took a mouthful and gulped it down. His face
scrunched up before relief settled into it. He took another
swig.

CAMELLE.
August, you don't have to do that . . .

August swallowed the last of the elixir and let out a
deep sigh. The others stared.

AUGUST.
What are you all looking at?
Get another bottle out!

SOLOMAN.
That's what I'm talking about!

AUGUST.
What would my mother think?

Soloman pulled a cork from another bottle with his
teeth.

SOLOMAN.
Doesn't matter. She isn't here, is she?

* * *

The funeral for Soloman's mother contained eight attendees: a six-year-old Soloman, his grandmother, his father, a fellow fisherman, the tailor whom his mother worked for, two other seamstresses, and the postman.

The small crowd made young Soloman very angry. He felt as though the whole world should have been standing in that humid cemetery, sweating through black fabric and scratching their ankles from unkempt grass. Didn't they know who she was? She could fix any broken clock, memorized the lyrics to every radio song, and arranged intricate fruit platters that resembled murals, for heaven's sake. Perhaps his father had forgotten to send out invitations. After all, Soloman had watched his mother comfort and service so many while she walked the earth, and yet, none of those people were in sight.

When the ceremony ended, he and his father walked home, hand in hand. Soloman didn't know why he'd expected something upon their return. He thought someone would paint the stones of their cottage walls his mother's favorite shade of yellow, or perhaps hang a banner with her name on it that could be seen from the sky.

Instead, the stones remained the color of ash, and her name was never spoken again. The seamstresses brought over warm meals for the first two weeks, but after that, no one seemed to remember Soloman's mother at all. Only his father showed any care. Years later, Soloman would still catch him staring at the dresses hanging in their wardrobe whenever he went to grab his coat.

*   *   *

CAMELLE.
Why don't we play a different game?

WINNIE.
I've an idea for someone brave.
I feel like causing a little harm.
Who's up for an arm-to-arm?

SOLOMAN.
Challenge accepted, Lady Sass.

Soloman left the wheel, grabbed an empty mop bucket, and turned it upside down. He poured some red into a cup.

SOLOMAN.
First arm down finishes the glass.

He placed his elbow onto the bucket as Winnie did the same.

WINNIE.
The name's Winnie,
and soon you'll be pitied.
I'm going to conquer you, my friend.

Soloman stopped. This was the first time that they had heard Winnie's name.
August calmly broke the silence.

AUGUST.
Shall Camelle and I bet on how it ends?

My money's on Winnie for this one.

Camelle chimed in for the rescue.

CAMELLE.
Then my bet's on Soloman!

Soloman grabbed Winnie's hand, making one joint fist. They wrestled for only a moment when Winnie cried out, clutching her stomach in pain.

AUGUST.
What did you do to her?!

SOLOMAN.
I . . . I'm not sure . . .

Winnie's forehead shined from sweat. She wiped her hands against her knees.

CAMELLE.
Perhaps you should take off your coat.

WINNIE.
No. I just need a moment alone.

She stood cautiously. Soloman's eyes flickered toward the money pile. August put his hand over it.

AUGUST.
You don't get to win by cheating.

SOLOMAN.
I never claimed to have beaten—

CAMELLE.
The bet's off. Nobody wins.

WINNIE.
It's fine, August. It wasn't him.
I'll see you all at dawn.
Don't kill each other while I'm gone.

*   *   *

When Soloman was a child, money only made him feel good. Whenever it came to him, it was a welcomed surprise—a silver coin from his father, two from his grandmother. All of which he would use on ice cream or toy boats or candy. He associated it with glee.

As he got older, however, he grew bitter toward it. Now that it was expected, it was never enough. No longer was it a nice surprise; it was only something always missing.

A wealthy man once told Soloman he was thinking of it all wrong.

"If you love it," he said, *"it will love you."*

This, of course, was easier said than done.

By the time he was ten, Soloman only had faint recollections of his mother. He remembered her cheeriness in hospital beds before she spent the rest of her days in his parents' bedroom. He remembered sharing pudding with her no matter which bed she was in. It wasn't until he grew up that he realized they had never stood a chance against the hospital bills. She had chosen to return home and spend her time there. She could have lived. She could have lived, but the world decided she wasn't enough for it.

And so, money became an old friend who'd stabbed Soloman in the back. He could not help but resent it. Yet, all the same, he had no choice but to keep chasing it. He needed its love desperately, no matter how many times it hurt him.

* * *

SOLOMAN.
I did nothing to her, I swear.

CAMELLE.
Soloman, there's no need to fear.
She was tired and lost control.
We know you wouldn't hurt a soul.

SOLOMAN.
Tell that to August, or your mother.

AUGUST.
How long have you both known each other?

SOLOMAN.
We don't need to get into the details.
You can ignore his question, Elle.

CAMELLE.
Since we were eight.

SOLOMAN.
Oh, that's great.
Ignore me, then. That's just fine.

AUGUST.
That's a long time.

CAMELLE.
Yes, it is. Quite long.

SOLOMAN.
Cheers. Let's move on.

CAMELLE.
We met in primary school.
The other children were a bit cruel.
My family was new to the town,
and folks didn't like my father around.
Anyway, on my walk one morning,
it starts to rain without warning.
My shoes are muddy, books soaked,
and as a supposed harmless joke,
some girls push me in a puddle.
I worry I'd get into trouble
for ruining my new books.
I pick them up to have a look
and begin shedding endless tears
when suddenly, an umbrella appears.
I glance up, and there he is.
He takes my books, and hands me his.

Soloman's fingers began to loosen on the wheel.

CAMELLE.
"I'm Soloman," he says to me.
I say mine, which he repeats.
It'll sound mad, but I swear to you . . .
The sun came out, the sky turned blue.
As soon as that boy said my name,
the clouds acted like they'd never rained.

August's curiosity deepened as he observed the two.

AUGUST.
What does your mother have to do with it?

Soloman's hands tightened again. He cleared his throat.

SOLOMAN.
She never liked me. Not one bit.

CAMELLE.
Soloman, that's simply not true.

SOLOMAN.
I was never good enough for you.

Camelle grew silent. Soloman looked away from her and kept his eyes on the sea.

AUGUST.
I apologize. I shouldn't have asked.

CAMELLE.
It's all right. The past is the past.

* * *

It was Soloman's last night in town before he was to leave for the academy. It was a given that he was to spend it with Camelle.

He arrived at her building at about eight o'clock. She opened the door wearing a mauve raincoat and ivory boots. A sadness washed over him, the stark realization that he would no longer see her every day. At that moment, he regretted ever distancing himself from her.

If there were any sadness on her end, Camelle certainly did not show it. She shut the door behind her and was strolling down the sidewalk before he could say hello.

They went out for a bite at a spot by the waterfront. Camelle chose a table in the corner farthest from the kitchen, where they could escape the noise of frying pans and shouting servers.

Soloman ordered a chowder for Camelle, counted the change in his pocket, and got himself a ginger beer. When she raised an eyebrow, he insisted he wasn't hungry.

They alternated between bits of conversation and silence, discussing little things like which students were staying and which were leaving town, how relieved the teachers looked on the last day of school.

Camelle couldn't finish her soup and told him to do it for her. He asked her if she wanted something else. She said no. He knew she was lying—that she knew how much change he had in his pocket and was sharing her meal with him.

When Soloman finished eating, he placed the change on the table and asked her to follow him. They went outside, and though the air had grown colder since they'd arrived, their bodies were two bonfires traveling across the shore.

He led her up the rocks hanging over the sea. She protested at first. It was late; her mother would worry. She gave in when he grasped her hand.

At the top, Soloman checked his watch. Right on time.

They looked below where his father's fishing vessel, along with a dozen others, parted the docks one by one. The boats sprinkled the sea with their lights, illuminating the dark waters like an oscillating night sky.

Then they had their first, and only, kiss. When it happened, it was not a surprise. For years, it had felt as though it would happen eventually. The excitement was not from the fact that it happened but when, and where, and how, because those were the only things they did not know.

Yet, just as quickly as passion washed over Soloman, so did the grief.

"Elle . . . I'll be gone a long time."

"I know, but we'll write."

"I just don't know what'll happen."

"What'll happen is you'll be a captain."

He had walked her back to her home. There, he expected a somber embrace, perhaps a bit of tears, but he didn't expect the smoke . . . the screams . . . his cowardice. She cried out for her mother. Was she out of the building? If they had arrived sooner, if he had taken her home when she'd asked . . .

She found her mother on a gurney. He hid behind a fire engine, skin itching from the blistering heat, heart thundering within his chest. As mother and daughter reached for each other's hands, he breathed a sigh of relief.

Through the flickering haze, orange as the sun, Soloman realized the harm he could have caused, of what little use he really was. He was an open flame in the idyllic garden of Camelle's life. She was better off without him, and though she anticipated letters, he decided then that he would not write.

Then he ran.

* * *

CAMELLE.
The days feel longer out here.
One can go mad when the water's so clear.
Does anyone know how long we've sailed for?

August walked over to the bow.

AUGUST.
Look! There seems to be shore.
Wait . . . haven't we seen that island?
Yes, there. The rocks shaped like lions!
How's that possible? We saw all these new things go by.

CAMELLE.
Were they new, or did we miss them the first time?

There was a silence where not even the water could
be heard.
August made his way back toward the others.

AUGUST.
Soloman, which direction have you been going?

SOLOMAN.
Whichever way the wind is blowing.

AUGUST.
. . . There hasn't been a breeze in days.

More silence followed, save for the soft thump of an
apricot falling from one of the trees on deck.

SOLOMAN.
Then we are, perhaps, in the same place . . .

CAMELLE.
Oh, dear.

AUGUST.
That's it! From now on, I steer!
I don't know what I was thinking,
giving the wheel to a man who'd been drinking.

He shoved Soloman aside.

SOLOMAN.
You know, I've had it with you, you pretentious—

AUGUST.
Don't bother, you're defenseless.

They charged at each other.

* * *

When Soloman first entered the maritime academy, he was so focused on the result, he never stopped to think about everything in between.

On the first day of class, he and the other boys were given a list of textbooks required. *"You'll find them at the bookshop in town,"* the instructor had told them.

When Soloman got to the shop, he was surprised to see each book cost nearly a day's worth of his father's wages. He certainly did not have enough to spend, nor did he want to ask his poor father for assistance, who had already taken loans from the bank to send Soloman to the academy in the first place.

Soloman tried the library but was told textbooks weren't available at libraries. There were new editions created each year that libraries just couldn't afford to keep up with. So, he went back to the store and slipped the books into his coat.

A week later, he got an evening job as a barkeep. Despite fooling the owner into thinking he was an expert, it was on this job that Soloman had his first drink.

Soloman had always known he needed a title to make money, though he never realized he had to have money to get a title.

* * *

SOLOMAN.
Go on! Let's see this through.
I've fought bigger things than you.

Soloman's back collided with the deck as August knocked him down. Puffs of dirt sputtered up from the ground as they scuffled.

CAMELLE.
Stop it! Stop it, now!
Winnie, help me with these clowns!

She turned to face Winnie, who had not moved the entire time, nor looked away from her book.

WINNIE.
I'm afraid they're all yours, little friend.
Aren't you curious how it'll end?

CAMELLE.
They'll kill each other, heaven forbid!
At this rate, I'll never reach the squid!

Winnie put down her book. Soloman and August stopped. The dust settled around them.

They all fixed their gaze on Camelle, who realized she had just made an awful mistake.

AUGUST.

You're here . . . to seek the same thing?

Soloman kicked August off him.

SOLOMAN.

We're obviously not on a boat to hunt something with wings.

AUGUST.

Mother of pearl spit!

SOLOMAN.

That's not really a saying, is it?

They both stood.

August clutched at two bleeding scrapes on the inside of his forearm. Soloman wiped a bead of sweat from his brow. Camelle began to cry.

CAMELLE.

Oh, what have I done?

WINNIE.

Well . . . *this* trip just got more fun.

AUGUST.

Right. It's clear we all want the squid for ourselves, but no one here should dare hurt anyone else.

CAMELLE.
How could you say such words?
To even consider that is absurd!
We're all good people, aren't we?

AUGUST.
I trust that we will be.

He gave Soloman a pointed look.

Soloman scoffed and went downstairs in a huff. He searched the cupboards for a bottle, but they had finished it all.

* * *

Three hundred and sixty. That's how many days on the water were required to graduate.

Soloman had never made it to day one.

It was the last written test that they were to take. There were to be sixty questions on safety procedures and hypotheticals. Soloman had studied for weeks, reviewing his textbooks behind the bar on slower days. He'd been scolded more than once by the owner, but he knew he'd never lose his job. His charm made him the customers' favorite, bringing bevies of women to the bar, often accompanied by more men.

Then the test came, and it was in a format he did not expect.

You see, if there was simply a blank space for him to fill in, he was sure whatever answer he'd written down would have sufficed. Instead, there were four answers which he was to choose from. This proved to be complicated, for the options provided were quite similar to each other.

The question asked for the best answer out of the four—not necessarily which was correct, but rather which was *most* correct, meaning they were all at least somewhat correct.

Soloman found something wrong in all four answers. For him, it was a matter of choosing not what felt most correct but what felt the least wrong. Not to mention, he was not a "possibilities" kind of fellow; in life, he always went with the first thing that came to mind. So, what was he to do when his first instinct was not one of the four options?

Needless to say, Soloman did not do well on the test.

Out of all the scenarios he had come up with in his head, Soloman never imagined flunking out of the academy, yet there he was. He found himself remaining in the town long after, as though unable to accept it. His father had begged him to come home, insisting he was forgiven for dropping out. Still, Soloman's shame made it impossible to face him. So, he wrote from time to time, letting him know he was all right.

Despite not being in school, Soloman frequented the parties. He'd scour them for free drinks and met various women from the nursing school across town who assumed he was one of the academy boys. He'd tell them his bunkmate was ill as an excuse to go to their dormitories instead of the dump he lived in. They never suspected anything unless they came looking for him at the academy, only to be told there was no one by that name.

One day, a girl invited Soloman to the town fair. She was a circus performer who frequently did juggling acts at the bar he worked in. She was reckless like he was, spoke without thinking, and had little care for others' opinions. Soloman quite liked that, so he agreed.

At the fair, they rode the Ferris wheel and shot darts at balloons. They guessed the correct weight of a pig (two hundred and eight kilograms) and won some cash. Soloman had never had a day so free of worry. He even thought of kissing her at the end of the evening.

They grew hungry and decided to spend their prize money on something to eat, so they made their way to a booth by the carousel.

The girl put in an order for cod and chips with a side of slaw.

As they stood there waiting for the food, Soloman had a sudden desire to leave. When their order arrived, he excused himself, ran right through the legs of a stilt walker, and exited the fair.

* * *

CAMELLE.
Soloman? Are you in here?
Must you always disappear?

Soloman didn't answer, checking empty cupboards twice as though some liquor would magically appear.

SOLOMAN.
That quack thinks I'm untrustworthy?
What about him? Who the blazes is he?
They'll desert us to get the squid,
or better yet throw us overboard. I know it.

CAMELLE.
Stop. They're not going to betray us.
We won't survive this without trust.

SOLOMAN.
Come now, Elle. Open your eyes.
People are full of nothing but lies.
You are so innocent, so sincere.
Too kind for this world, I fear.

CAMELLE.
Everyone has a bit of good in them!
Even if they don't, I won't succumb.
I don't care what others are like—
only who I am in this life.

SOLOMAN.
You haven't changed a bit.

CAMELLE.
Do you still like it?

Soloman smiled at her, memories dancing before
them like fireflies. He watched as the pupils of her eyes
began to bloom, and for a moment, it felt as though the
picture he had so longed to paint was complete upon a
canvas. Yet, the canvas hung from a bent nail, gently
swinging against a rotting wall. There was more to be done.

SOLOMAN.
We can't trust what the others will do.

CAMELLE.
You trust me, don't you?
I promise there's no need for hostility.

SOLOMAN.
There's a fine line between kindness and stupidity.

Soloman regretted his words as soon as he saw the wet glow of her eyes. Their blossoms were now drowning beneath an endless rain, and he was reminded of the severity of his influence.

SOLOMAN.
I didn't mean that you were st— No!

Camelle fled.

SOLOMAN.
Elle, forgive me. Don't go.

He tossed an empty bottle at a wall, letting it shatter. The blistering heat of his self-loathing threatened to set the ship ablaze.

*　*　*

Soloman had experienced dozens of kisses during his days, but there was one he was never able to shake. Whenever he closed his eyes, he would remember the smell of the sea, the ringing bells of the fishing boats. How it felt both thrilling and soothing, dangerous and safe. He wondered if it would always be that way with her or if that flame would eventually fade. Though he feared the latter, he needed to find out, for it was the last memory of comfort that he had.

After six years of being away, Soloman had decided to return home. However, his guilt haunted him. Had it been long enough for her to forgive him? How could he justify what he did? And how would he explain leaving the academy? She would be so disappointed.

If Soloman was not enough to be a captain, what made him enough for Camelle? He would be a fool to think he could fit into her life now. If he didn't have a name or title, he would need something else. He needed something, or he was nothing but dust.

That was when Soloman sought the squid.

* * *

August stared at the parallel scrapes across his arm. He took off the scarf enveloping his neck and tightened it around the wound. He had almost lost sight of what he came for—but not anymore. No more games, no more drinks, no more distractions.

In the distance, burning clouds drifted over the watery home of the thing that would be the end of his battles. The pain in his chest had subsided for brief moments, but now it coursed through him again. His shoulders curled, his back bent, and his soul was hollow. He looked to Winnie, who glanced back at him before disappearing through the trees.

August took the wheel.

Part II:
August

August Norwood was prompt to everything. His closet was organized by shades of brown, and each of his socks always had a partner. He could not and would not stand the irresponsible. He found them inconsiderate and the reason for most of his problems.

August was autumn. In the same way a compass always points north, he could not help but adhere to his home. The Norwoods lived in a manor across from their twenty-four acres of aspen trees, which they used to produce matches at their factory downtown. August spent most of his days assisting the family business consisting of his parents along with his father's five brothers and their wives. To the Norwoods, family was the most important thing there was.

"Nothing is as dense as blood," his folks would say, to which August and his brother Reed would nod in obedience.

If August were a sparrow, then Reed would be a cardinal. They were nearly identical twins, apart from Reed's locks evoking enchanting flames beside August's brown curls. He greeted the world before August did and continued to do so throughout their childhood.

Reed dominated every space he occupied. He possessed valor, loyalty, and a willingness to stand up for others. He was skilled in the factory and made it a lively place to work. Unlike those who developed insecurities as a result of their more beloved siblings, August never minded the attention Reed received. He felt safe in his brother's presence—relieved he wouldn't have to exert much energy, as Reed had enough for them both.

*   *   *

AUGUST.
We should all gather and talk.

August looked through the woodland deck as Winnie emerged with a different book in her hand.

WINNIE.
Perhaps after Soloman cools off.

AUGUST.
I understand that they have history,
but he strikes me as being slippery.
Do you think he feels the same about her?

WINNIE.
He cares just as much, I'm sure.
People express themselves in different ways.
She walks a straight line; he lives in a maze.

Winnie thumbed through the pages of her book.

AUGUST.
You read quite a lot.

WINNIE.
It's all I've got.

Camelle ran toward them with a glisten in her eyes.
August rubbed his neck. Tears were not something
he was used to being around; his family never allowed them.

AUGUST.
Camelle? Are you all right?

CAMELLE.
I've made a mess, haven't I?
An absolute mess!

WINNIE.
Yes.

August gave Winnie a look.

AUGUST.
You were just speaking the truth.
Of course you want the squid. We all do.

CAMELLE.
But I shouldn't have said it out loud.
Things will be delicate between us now.
We'll see each other as competition,

and I'm the one who put us in this position!

Soloman came up to the deck. August looked down
at the floor. He wasn't proud of how he had acted, despite
Soloman's blunders.

SOLOMAN.
Elle, please come talk to me.

CAMELLE.
I'm done speaking.

There was a strained silence. August shifted his foot.

AUGUST.
Right. Since we're all here,
we'll hold a meeting while I steer.
Let us decide who'll get the squid
in the case that we do find it.

WINNIE.
Shouldn't it be whoever finds it first?

CAMELLE.
That'd just make things worse.
We'd tear each other into bits!
Isn't it best that we share it?

SOLOMAN.
We don't know where it is, or what it looks like.
For all we know, we're wasting our time!

WINNIE.
It's warm, apparently. I've heard that much.

CAMELLE.
There's enough of it for all of us.

AUGUST.
One finds it by working hard.

SOLOMAN.
Those who've found it are liars and frauds.

AUGUST.
Why are you here if you don't believe it to be true?

SOLOMAN.
Because I don't know what else to do!

The others had never heard Soloman raise his voice before.

CAMELLE.
Look, we'll figure it out when the time comes.
If anyone could find the squid, we're the ones.

WINNIE.
Thank you, Miss Ambition.
You provide much assistance.

Camelle began to droop again. August thought about what she'd said. He didn't have the strength to contend. Perhaps it was more suitable that they hunted together.

AUGUST.
Whoever is first to spot it in the water
should do their duty to inform the others.
We'll have an equal chance of catching it
as long as we keep that promise.

He extended an arm. Winnie hesitated, then placed
hers on his. Camelle dried her eyes and put hers on
Winnie's. They all turned to Soloman.

SOLOMAN.
You've got to be kidding me.

The others remained unmoving. Soloman sighed
and placed his hand on Camelle's. A blustery wind rushed
through them.

AUGUST.
Now, someone, fix us something to eat.

* * *

Every morning, Tuls Norwood drove the daily
lumber to the factory downtown where Lottygun Norwood
put it through the shredder. Once the aspen wood was cut
into splints, Edger Norwood soaked them in ammonium
phosphate to prevent the matches from having afterglow.
The soaked splints were handed over to Holst Norwood,
who ran a machine that dipped the tips into wax. After the
dipped matchsticks dried, they were inserted into boxes of
forty-eight. A whistling Warth Norwood would place these

matchboxes into larger boxes, and Evyn Norwood would then stack those into crates while humming her favorite tune.

On one such day, Edger Norwood poured a sack of splints into the ammonium phosphate like he always did. This time however, a single splint fell to the floor before making it into the barrel. It remained there for about an hour until Pedir Norwood, in charge of delivering the crates to local shops, came strolling into the factory to use the commode. On his way, he felt something beneath his shoe, lifted it, and saw the stray splint. Thinking he was doing the responsible thing, Pedir picked it up and tossed it into the dipping machine, where it received a cardinal-red wax tip.

* * *

SOLOMAN.
I can whip something up for us all.
Perhaps some cod, chips, and slaw.
I'm not a bad cook, myself.
How does that sound, Elle?

Camelle didn't answer.

WINNIE.
I'll assist you, out of concern.
Wouldn't want anything to get burned.

AUGUST.
Go on and leave a plate here
if you all want to dine downstairs.

CAMELLE.
None of that nonsense.
You're to join us, August.

Camelle set down blankets by the wheel.

SOLOMAN.
Well, isn't that great?

CAMELLE.
I'll grab us some plates.

Camelle followed Soloman and Winnie below deck.
When they reached the kitchen, she immediately began
pulling plates from the cupboards.

SOLOMAN.
Elle . . . Earlier, I didn't mean to say—

There was a clang as Camelle tossed silverware onto
a stack of plates and exited in a huff.
Soloman sighed.

WINNIE.
What did you do to her, anyway?

SOLOMAN.
You'd be sorry you asked.
Let's just focus on the task.

WINNIE.
There isn't any cod.

SOLOMAN.
What have we got?

WINNIE.
Carrots, squash, an onion or two.
Looks like you're making soup.

SOLOMAN.
Great. Once again, I'll disappoint her.
She's probably crying on his shoulder.

WINNIE.
Afraid you'll have competition?

SOLOMAN.
Who wouldn't want a man of his description?

* * *

Norwood Matches had been in business for four generations, though its story began much earlier. It was said that August's ancestors had planted a single aspen tree on their property, not knowing how heartily it would spread. Apparently, aspens stem from one root system and can grow as quickly as twenty-four inches per year. The Norwoods eventually had an entire forest of identical trees they didn't know what to do with.

August always found it extraordinary how much wealth had derived from a single tree. The family property grew and grew until it was passed down to his father, the eldest son at the time. Otto Norwood was stern about keeping the business within the family, despite the incompetence of some members.

August knew his father believed Reed had more promise than he did—that his brother could eventually run the family business and help it thrive. Though he had no interest in being a leader, especially for something as mundane as a match company, it still hurt to know his father did not think him capable.

August may not have been the brightest or had half as much daring as Reed, but he wasn't as careless as his uncles, aunts, or cousins. Regardless, he was always the one everyone seemed most disappointed in. The act of criticizing August was entertainment to the Norwoods. They teased him constantly, as though they enjoyed the sound of him crunching beneath their feet.

* * *

CAMELLE.
I don't know why I keep letting him do this to me.

As Camelle set plates down on the blankets, August could tell her mind was elsewhere.

AUGUST.
We can't control our hearts, can we?

He watched as she placed two forks beside one plate and two knives beside another. She realized her mistake, shook her head, and rearranged them. Then she took a seat, and he could feel the weight of her pain spilling onto the blanket.

AUGUST.
You mustn't let him break you down.
He'd be lucky to have you, not the other way 'round.

He sensed a drop of sadness fall upon the petals of
her heart.

CAMELLE.
August, would you say I'm naïve?

AUGUST.
Is that what you believe?

CAMELLE.
It wasn't what he said that made me blue.
It was the fear that it could be true.
How does one stay kind without ignorance?

AUGUST.
By being filled with bitterness.
I'm afraid I'm not much help on the subject.
If I come off poised, I promise I'm a wreck.

August was relieved to see the corners of Camelle's
mouth turn upward.

CAMELLE.
True. I see the way you look at her.

AUGUST.
Who? What? Don't be absurd.

CAMELLE.
You do think me a fool, then!
She has you practically drooling!
I'd like to express my sentiment, if you don't mind.

AUGUST.
Please do, for I fear I'm blind.

CAMELLE.
You can't keep doing what you're doing.
It's just— The constant wooing and pursuing . . .
You're so serious. Let yourself go!

AUGUST.
Being serious is all I've ever known.

CAMELLE.
Winnie could use a balance. Someone fun.

AUGUST.
Right. Someone like Soloman?

CAMELLE.
Too fun. All I'm saying is, I think we'd prefer
if she warmed up to you, not for you to freeze up to her.

AUGUST.
I'm not sure that's much help.

CAMELLE.
Don't try so hard or you'll hurt yourself.

AUGUST.
I'm afraid I still need a bit of healing.

CAMELLE.
I sure understand that feeling.

AUGUST.
You deserve better than him, you know.

CAMELLE.
If only his charm wasn't irresistible.

AUGUST.
At least you've stayed true to your nature.
Life has taken a toll on my behavior.
I used to dream of so much . . .

CAMELLE.
That's the beauty of you, August.
You'd give up parts of yourself, your deepest desires,
if it would make those you love a little brighter.

August felt the ache spread through his chest again.
He was relieved when Camelle went on.

CAMELLE.
Give her time. She'll see what you bring.
Although, there is one thing . . .
She isn't very fond of me.

AUGUST.
I'm sure it's just the sea.

Nausea can make anyone irritable.
Her words aren't personal.

CAMELLE.
Although you think me unwise,
I do appreciate the effort of your lies.

August offered a playful bow.

CAMELLE.
That's it! There you go!
That's the side she should know!

* * *

"Why don't you ever smile, dear?" his mother said
once when he was ten.

She sat on his bed, sewing his name on the inside of
his sport coat. August stood beside her, staring at himself in
the mirror. She had put him in his fanciest vest and trousers,
with a tie tightened around his neck. Reed had finished
dressing long before him and was already greeting guests at
the door.

*"This dinner is very important. The people here will
give your father money, but only if they like our family. You
must be polite. It's no place to fool around. Is that
understood?"*

August looked at the floor. Guests always made
remarks about him, how he was peculiar and quieter than
Reed. He never knew how to act in social situations.
Whenever someone addressed him, he would try
responding the way his father would, or nod his head in

agreement the way Reed did. He clung onto the people around him, changed his colors to match theirs. Red, orange, yellow—he was whatever shade they wanted him to be.

His mother cupped his chin and turned his head toward her.

"You wouldn't have anything if it weren't for the blood and sweat of your father and the generations before him. Don't be ungrateful."

She held up the needle in her hand and snapped the thread with her teeth.

"There you go. Now the maids won't confuse it with your brother's."

* * *

CAMELLE.
Here she comes!
Remember . . . be fun.

Camelle stood and brushed off her worries. Winnie wandered toward the wheel as Camelle passed her.

WINNIE.
Where are you off to? Cat stuck in a tree?

CAMELLE.
Good evening to you too, Winnie.

August gave Camelle a look of apology before she retreated below deck. He turned to Winnie, who seemed to be fashioning some sort of spear. He stared as she sharpened the end of a branch with a knife.

AUGUST.
I do hope that's for fish.

WINNIE.
If that's what you wish.

AUGUST.
Are you this cold all the time?

WINNIE.
Just trying to survive.

AUGUST.
You don't have to tease Camelle, you know.

WINNIE.
Oh, rubbish. She'll let it go.
Besides, Soloman wouldn't call you nice.
Perhaps you should take your own advice.

She stopped sharpening the branch to pull a bread roll from her pocket. August watched in awe as Winnie deftly shoved the entire roll into her mouth.

AUGUST.
He starts it most of the time.

Winnie lectured him with her mouth full.

WINNIE.
Two wongs don' make a—

AUGUST.
All right!
You win. I'll be kind, if I must.
There's just something about him that I don't trust.
People like that only cause trouble for others.
They have their fun and let everyone else suffer.

Winnie continued through her chews.

WINNIE.
Soloman's no different from anyone else.
We all can only trust ourselves.

AUGUST.
Have you no friends, nor allies nor lovers?

WINNIE.
Friends are but enemies undiscovered.

AUGUST.
Were you always this tenacious and tough,
this sullen and sour, this bitter and rough?

WINNIE.
There was a time my heart could ache,
long before it was left to break.
They taught me to caution where I swim.
I just never thought to be wary of them.

AUGUST.
Winnie, if only you knew—

WINNIE.
Please. I'm not one to be rescued.

AUGUST.
I don't know what you mean, I'm afraid.

WINNIE.
You still think I'm to be played.
Step one: Be the understanding charmer.
Get the girl to drop her armor.

AUGUST.
That's not at all what I'm trying to do!
. . . What's step two?

WINNIE.
You don't have to do this around me.
This act of who you think you should be.

August looked at the woman before him—cheeks inflated with bread, hands coarser than the bark they chipped at. He knew then that they would become dear friends.

* * *

When August and Reed were young, a governess would come to the manor to educate them in all the necessary disciplines at home. The governess had a daughter their age who did her lessons with them as well. The girl took a liking to August, which surprised him considering most gravitated toward Reed. He and the girl would play in the yard or run miles across the estate, and she was also the only worthy chess opponent he could find. August thought it was nice having a companion other than his brother.

One afternoon, after spending the morning going over their arithmetic, August and the girl explored the edges of the aspen forest. They carved into the tall white trunks, darkening them with swordsmen and beasts and sea creatures.

August was just finishing up etching himself as an adult into one trunk, wearing a striped bow tie, when the girl decided to add to the portrait. She told him not to look as she chipped away at the bark, the peels falling to the ground. When she finished, he saw that she had carved herself beside him, holding his hand, wearing a veil upon her head.

Suddenly, August felt bothered in a way he had never been before. He had the urge to run and crawl into his bed. He wished he was one of the ants scurrying across their fantastical drawings, or a bird flying across the vermillion sky above them, or anything other than himself.

He smiled politely and let the girl drag him through the aspens for another hour. Ever since then, he would pretend to be ill whenever she wanted to go out to the yard, or play only half a game of chess with her before resigning.

When it came time for them to attend school, August begged his folks not to make him go. Mr. and Mrs. Norwood couldn't seem to parse why their son was so opposed to the idea.

"Don't you want to make friends?" they asked him.

They had expected him to look forward to being out
of the house. After all, Reed would often be caught playing
ball or jacks with the other boys in town. To August,
however, being around others his age sounded like the worst
thing in the world. He assured his parents that he found it
much easier to concentrate on his studies when there
weren't any distractions.

After much debate, the Norwoods agreed to hire
him a tutor, while Reed went off to school as planned.

* * *

AUGUST.
You think I'm putting on an act?

WINNIE.
I know it for a fact.
It comes off a bit desperate.
I can't say I'm fond of it.

AUGUST.
Have you ever bitten your tongue?
In all your life . . . even just once?

Winnie finished chewing.

WINNIE.
Yes, just now, with that bread.
Tell me, is my tongue red?

AUGUST.
Ah, I see. She taunts me now.

I'm sure you're quite proud.
I won't compete with your wit.

WINNIE.
That was good, wasn't it?

Winnie held up her sharpened branch and examined it in the light.

AUGUST.
Look, I appreciate you trying to guide me,
but I don't know what it is you think I'm hiding.
I would be thrilled to tell you if I could.

Winnie put down her creation. She stood and began hacking another branch off a tree with the knife.

WINNIE.
Who are you, August Norwood?

* * *

August met Leo on a Sunday morning when he was struck by a desperate craving for pecan pie.

He had woken with a crick in his neck. His body seemed to have stopped cooperating as soon as he'd turned eighteen, unlike Reed's, which seemed to only get stronger. Although August could hear the maids preparing breakfast, he decided to take it upon himself to visit the new bakery downtown. He made sure to slip out through the kitchen so the rest of the house wouldn't notice him leaving.

When August stepped into the empty shop, he was greeted by classical music blaring from a radio behind the counter. A man with intention in his eyes and flour on his nose wiped his hands on his apron.

"Welcome to Bach & Bake!
We have pastries, bread, and cake.
Though we may be new in town,
our desserts are the best around!
Anything catch your eye?"

"Do you happen to have pecan pie?"

"For you, I'll make one right away.
That is, if you don't mind staying."

"Oh, no. A lemon scone will be plenty."

"It'd be no worry. The shop's empty."

"Well, all right then. I'll pay you double
since you're going through all the trouble."

"Double for pie? That would be a thievin'.
Buy me a coffee and we'll call it even."

Leo liked string instruments, museums, and mint leaves in his tea. The walls of his apartment were covered with recipes and postcards. He made breakfast every morning and baked dessert every evening. He never got angry, except whenever an egg rolled off the counter, to which he would shout, *"Mother of pearl spit!"*

More importantly, Leo had a way of making August feel seen—that he wasn't just living in Reed's shadow. He adored August's need for perfection, consistently praising him for his organization. He'd tease him for the various shades of brown in his wardrobe and gifted him orange hats and scarves. Leo noticed things no one else ever did. He knew exactly what August liked and what he didn't. To Leo, he was never August Norwood. He was only August.

Yet, what August loved most was how he never apologized for who he was. Leo was filled with a golden light and refused to let anyone dim it. He took only the most important things seriously and found everything else amusing. It was easy to fall for him, and August did so instantly.

* * *

SOLOMAN.
There's been a change of plans!

Soloman came up the deck carrying a pot, eyes fixed on his creation so as to not spill a drop. Camelle followed close behind with bowls and spoons.

August was surprised to find himself disappointed by the interruption. A part of him had hoped to answer Winnie's question.

WINNIE.
Do you need a hand?

SOLOMAN.
No need. I've got this.

Soloman set the pot down in the center of the blankets. Camelle reset the area, clearing away the plates and knives.

AUGUST.
What happened to fish?

SOLOMAN.
As it turns out . . . there are none.

WINNIE.
If we stop at an island, I can spear some.

AUGUST.
There hasn't been an island in weeks.
We'll need to gather fruit from the trees.

CAMELLE.
I'll make jam for the bread rolls.

SOLOMAN.
Now, then, give me your bowls.

He scooped the orange medley into each bowl, comfort wafting into their noses. Camelle brought one to August.

CAMELLE.
So? Were you fun?

AUGUST.
Not even once.

CAMELLE.
How will you ever win her heart?

SOLOMAN.
Quit whispering so we can start!

They had their first spoonfuls, and their tongues overflowed with flavor and spices as the ship rocked them gently. They allowed themselves to rest in the silence that followed.

WINNIE.
This is the longest I haven't been alone.

Though the others didn't know what to say, they appreciated Winnie's remark just the same. August glanced at her from the wheel, hoping to receive more fragments of her story.

They received nothing else.

CAMELLE.
This is the longest I've been away from home.

August took in the mixture on his spoon twice before setting it down.

AUGUST.
Did you never travel as a child?

CAMELLE.
Not more than a few miles.
I don't think I was allowed.

My mother didn't like to leave the house,
and I never thought to do it on my own.
I suppose I can now that I'm grown.

AUGUST.
What about you, Soloman?

SOLOMAN.
Quite the opposite.
I haven't been home in a long time.

He avoided Camelle's eyes.

AUGUST.
Right. Well . . . let us dine.

They slurped their supper until the sun hugged the
sea and spilled into the sky an enchanting red. When they
were done, their bellies were full of warmth and familiarity.

AUGUST.
I know I have been spiteful,
but Soloman, this was delightful.

Soloman tipped an invisible hat.

CAMELLE.
You've learned a lot over the years.

SOLOMAN.
Cheers.

AUGUST.
Right, then. None of us want to be starving,
so we should clean and begin harvesting.

SOLOMAN.
I'm so stuffed, I can barely think.
It's people like you who get me to drink.
Say, Winnie, where did you find grapes before?

Winnie licked her spoon ravenously.

WINNIE.
Grapes? I can't be sure.
I don't remember having any.

SOLOMAN.
We did. You threw them at me.

Soloman scratched his head as Winnie shrugged.

CAMELLE.
May we wait a little, August?
I think we're all exhausted.

August left the wheel and began scouring the deck
for buckets.

AUGUST.
Play and pleasure must always be earned.
Hop to! The lazy bird loses the worm.

* * *

"Can you move any slower, Leo?
We've only got two hours 'til the show.
It'll be forty minutes to the restaurant,
another sixteen to sit where we want.
Factor in the twelve of waiting,
at least another thirty-two for eating . . .
That's twenty to get to the opera house!"

"Relax. It's in the same part of town.
It'll take no more than eight to get to it."

"We'll need another eight for tickets!"

"Quit worrying, I've already got those.
You're not the only one who's responsible."

"What? When did you get that done?"

"August, trust someone else for once.
Besides, I'm four whole years older.
Things should rest on my shoulders."

Leo took time with his roasted pheasant as August devoured half his dish of bread pudding, which predictably caused a lecture from Leo about wasting food. After furiously flagging down the waiter, they made their way through town. The summer evening allowed for a walk without coats, though August still had a scarf Leo had gifted him wrapped loosely around his neck.

When they reached the end of their path, sirens deafened their harmony. A haze filled the air, and a flood of people hindered their way forward.

"Let's see what this is all about.
They'll let us through, no doubt."

"August. The smoke's giving me a cough."

August pushed through the crowd. Leo reluctantly squeezed past bodies, apologizing to frowning faces and trying not to lose him. They reached the front.

"I'm sorry, sir. This road's blocked off."

"We're on our way to the opera house."

"I'm afraid you'll have to go around.
There's been a fire, you see."

"Around? We'll be late to our seats!"

Leo grabbed August's arm.

"August, please. You must give in.
It's a fire. You won't win."

He pulled him out of the crowd.

"Is this show really important?"

"The tickets are all sorted!"

"There'll be other chances. Let's walk.
We'll forget the opera and just talk."

"Walk? To where? Wh— Are you sure?"

"Have you never simply taken a walk before?"

Leo took August's hand and the stress that had been swirling in August's chest blew away with the wind. He felt himself grasping onto whatever pieces of Leo's soul it could hold. Their fingers intertwined, and the hollowness he had endured his entire life, the belief that something was wrong with him, crumbled into specks between their palms.

In August's moment of ecstasy, a glob of spit landed on his shoes. A man called them words that had never reached August's ears until that moment. August let go of Leo's hand, the calm escaping him. Leo paid no attention to the man. He simply put his hands in his pockets and watched as August's mind became disquiet again.

"Leo, I don't think I have the guts.
This world just isn't meant for us."

"One day, it won't be meant for them."

"And what are we to do until then?
People know of me in this town.
If we're to do this, it can't get out.
Could you really live with that forever?"

Leo said nothing at first. His hands remained in his pockets as he faced the sea. It wasn't in Leo's nature to hide who he was; August knew that. The leaves of his heart withered as he waited for an answer. A train came roaring down the tracks beside them, blocking their view of the water.

Leo turned to him, shouting against the chugging wheels.

"Could you live with a man who's just a baker?
The most I'll ever own is a storefront."

August studied the conviction in Leo's eyes and the way his hair danced as railroad cars sped behind him in a blur.

He shouted back.

"How else will I get custard tarts whenever I want?"

They grinned at each other, clearing the haze between them. The train whistled as it faded into the distance.

"Then let us hold on to each other."

"All right. I'll tell my brother."

* * *

The four reached their arms above their heads, picking fruit from the trees. When they could reach no more, they climbed. As they scaled branch after branch, they looked out onto the ocean and saw farther than they ever had before.

August calculated the amount of fruit harvested as they collected them, scribbling on paper with one hand and steering with the other. Despite the others' advice that he get some rest, his nose remained hidden in the page.

They harvested each day, gathering enough to last them through the cold. And when the leaves began to fall and the sea turned shades of amber, they climbed the highest sail and plucked the last piece of fruit.

AUGUST.
Have we gathered enough food?

SOLOMAN.
Yes, we should be good.
This will feed us for a while.

CAMELLE.
What happened to the other pile?
There was another one just here.
Now it's gone and disappeared.

AUGUST.
Did you sort by ripeness like I advised?

CAMELLE.
Yes, there just seems to be less than I realized.

WINNIE.
Don't worry, princess. We have enough.

Winnie had gathered a heap of grapevines and was weaving some sort of basket.

AUGUST.
We'll divide it evenly among us.

August furrowed his brow as he stared at his
calculations. Unfortunately, the only thing that wasn't neat
about him was his handwriting. He tried forcing his mind to
function, but it refused, giving into the heaviness that
consumed him. He tossed his pen aside.

SOLOMAN.
Fantastic. Now, who's up for games?
I'm ready to put you all to shame.

AUGUST.
Not so fast.
There'll be no more of that.
Take these piles below deck
and get yourselves some needed rest.
You've all been working for hours.

Soloman rolled his eyes. As he and Camelle headed
downstairs, Winnie approached August and handed him the
silk satchel.

WINNIE.
These may return to your trousers.
I haven't been nauseous lately.

AUGUST.
You've gotten used to the sea!

Winnie didn't answer. August placed the satchel in his pocket. It was true that he liked the smell of mint leaves, but only because they reminded him of the way Leo drank his tea.

He watched as Winnie weaved her basket. They were alone again. He would tell her now.

*   *   *

Ever since they were teenagers, August would witness his brother take a different girl out on the town every other week. August often wondered how Reed managed to go through so many without upsetting any of them. He always expected weeping schoolgirls to pound on the gates of their estate or storm into their factory someday, but none ever did.

By the time they were twenty, Reed had so many women around him, August believed his brother had no real interest in anyone at all. Their folks seemed to grow impatient. The Norwoods had never been shy about wanting their children to marry well, and they clearly placed the most hope in Reed. Every evening, their father would press him about it at the dinner table.

"How do you like the physician's daughter, Reed?" he'd say. *"She's grown to be a pretty one. I hear she's quite skilled in sewing. She'd make a great wife."*

Reed would merely nod and stuff his mouth with a large bite of his food.

When August eventually told his brother about Leo, Reed encouraged him to invite him over for dinner. August expressed doubts in introducing him to the family, but Reed assured him that there would be no trouble and he'd take care of it if there was.

August was astonished when Reed proved to be correct. The Norwoods loved Leo. He humored their mother with stories of travel and talked business with their father, he had a playful retort for every jab their uncles made, and to top it all off he always brought over desserts, which made their aunts and cousins swoon.

As years passed, Leo grew to belong to the family behind closed doors. He became known as the Norwoods' baker, and no one batted an eye whenever he entered the property. This arrangement also turned out well for Leo, for it brought more customers to his shop.

All the while, Reed seemed not only thrilled for August but relieved that the focus was no longer on his own romantic life.

* * *

Winnie placed her finished basket beneath a tree. August cleared his throat.

AUGUST.
I . . . I'd like to answer your question.

Camelle appeared, holding glass jars in each hand.

CAMELLE.
The fruits are all stored in the kitchen!
I've kept some frozen, some in cans.
I'm going to start making the jam.
Do you both prefer peach or apricot?

Or I could use everything we've got!
Should I just make one of each?

August massaged his forehead.

AUGUST.
Sure, yes. Apricot, cherry, peach . . .
Make whatever jam you think is best.
And didn't I say to get some rest?
Fill two of each, then it's off to bed.

Camelle retreated gleefully. Winnie gave August a
look.

WINNIE.
"She's not that aggravating," he said.

AUGUST.
Fine! She does have a lot of fervor,
but that's only a reason to envy her.

WINNIE.
Is that how you feel about Soloman?

August thought for a moment. It was true. Something
about the man's carefree nature irked him—the way he acted
as though all was great and nothing in the world needed
fixing. August was ashamed he had given in to drinking away
his troubles. He refused to let Soloman influence him again.

WINNIE.
Perhaps we wish we could be like them.

AUGUST.
You know, I've been a poor sport since I was young,
and whenever I seemed down in the dumps,
my brother would always attempt to make me laugh
by tossing me over his shoulder so I hung down his back.
He'd say, "If being right-side up makes you frown,
then try living your life upside-down!"

He noticed something blue in Winnie's smile—a
familiar sorrow.

AUGUST.
Sometimes I lie upon the floor
with my legs against the wall.
I look up at the ceiling,
and it's like I can feel him.

* * *

On their twenty-fourth birthday, August and Reed's
father gave them a pair of motorbikes as a gift. The two went
for a ride on the main road just outside the Norwood estate.
The sun had set, and there hadn't been any passing cars for
miles. In fact, they were only two minutes from home when
Reed was killed instantly by a driver who had been drinking.
That was when August began hating the
irresponsible.
After Reed's death, August began to feel the weight
of being less than his brother. He tried to be useful to the
company, cutting lumber with his father and helping his
mother with the accounting. Yet, no matter who he was with,

they wore disappointment on their faces, and every moment of silence from them was like an axe against his chest.

As a result, August presented a manufactured version of himself to his family—one he knew they were capable of understanding. He accepted the fact that they would never fully know who he was, because they didn't have the ability to see what was there. They could only ever see what was missing.

He was never brave enough to ask them the question that haunted his mind, for he felt he already knew the answer.

* * *

WINNIE.
I'm sorry. I'm unwell again.
I'll be gone for just a minute.

Winnie began picking leftover grapevines from off the floor.

AUGUST.
Can I help with anything?

WINNIE.
Just keep your eyes on the sea.

Soloman appeared, stumbling back as Winnie sped by him. He peered at the vines in her arms.

SOLOMAN.
Is she making things to kill us with?

She hasn't caught a single fish.
I can't help but assume the worst.

AUGUST.

I hope she starts with you first.
Now, why is everybody awake?
Does no one listen to anything I say?

SOLOMAN.

First, you make us work when we're tired.
Now you send us to bed when we're wired.
I haven't been able to sleep a wink
ever since we finished the drinks.
My head hurts. I'm sure it's a fever.
I can't keep anything down, either.

AUGUST.

All the more reason to get some rest.
Besides, you got yourself into this mess.
Only you can get yourself out of it.
It won't help to throw a fit.

SOLOMAN.

Relax. I'm about to head in now.
And you're one to talk, old grouch.
You look even more weary than I did.
Quite determined to find that squid.
Trying to find it first, aren't you?

August realized that he was standing the same way
Soloman did, with his back straight and chin pointed up. He
hunched his shoulders again.

AUGUST.
We made a promise, one that I plan to stick to.

SOLOMAN.
Ah, a man of honor, he is.
He has our trust, but we must earn his.
What are you scribbling, anyway?
How much fruit is there to calculate?

AUGUST.
It seems Camelle was right before.
We picked more than we have stored.
I can't seem to find the missing bit.
Do you know anything about it?

No matter how many times he tried to bite his
tongue, August could not seem to stop accusing Soloman of
things. It was the only way he knew how to distance himself
from him.

SOLOMAN.
Never did I give you reason not to trust.
I've done all you asked. Was that not enough?
And yet, in a way . . . I understand.
The world can be a slippery land.
It must be hard, others knowing your name.
You never know what they're trying to gain.
Do you ever feel trapped by what you come from?

August didn't answer, fazed by the response. An
anger festered inside him, one that visited him often in the
aftermath of his brother's death. Sometimes, the urge to

destroy everything in sight consumed him, the desire to make them all as broken as he felt, but the civility that had been embedded in him since he was a child never allowed him that release.

SOLOMAN.

If you do, you're not the only one.
I'll leave you alone now, since you despise me.
Though, who doesn't? Can't say it's surprising.

AUGUST.

That's what you'll do? Go off and dwell?
Right. While you're feeling sorry for yourself,
there's a woman whose heart expected more.
Don't you think she's worth fighting for?

SOLOMAN.

You don't know a thing about where we've stood.

AUGUST.

I know she sees more in you than I ever could.
Do you not realize how lucky you are,
that you can run toward love whenever you want?
The rest of us can't say the same.
If you feel trapped, only you're to blame.

SOLOMAN.

Who are you to say that I can't dwell?
You've never had to live without wealth.
For all you know, love could be much harder
when a Norwood isn't your father.

* * *

Leo suggested the two of them go on a trip together. It had been a month since Reed's passing, and he thought perhaps it would be best for August to leave the estate for a while. Working at the factory wasn't doing him any good, and the grief had taken a toll on his health. Perhaps a change in scenery would clear his head.

August agreed and said he would inform his family that evening.

When dinner came, the Norwoods ate in silence as they had done for a month. Halfway through his pot roast, August mustered up the courage to speak.

"Leo and I are going on a trip.
It will only be for a bit."

His aunts and uncles looked at his folks with concern. His cousin Evyn looked down at her plate.

August's father folded his napkin and cleared his throat.

"With your brother gone," he said, *"it is now your duty to marry and have a son."*

A single teardrop fell into August's pot roast.

"We all wish things could have gone another way," his mother added.

And so August realized that what the Norwoods cared more about than family was the family name.

* * *

August composed himself as Winnie returned. Soloman pushed by her as he left, causing her to raise her brow.

WINNIE.

Has something been addressed?

AUGUST.

I might have said things that I now regret.

He took a breath. The air was crisp, and it reminded him of days from his childhood when he and Reed would enjoy warm spiced apple brews in their yard.

AUGUST.

I'd like to address your previous question.
You were right that I had false intentions.
You see, my brother died not long ago.
His name was Reed, and he was my hero.

He unwrapped the scarf from his arm and ran his thumb over the slow-healing lines.

AUGUST.

With him gone, I'm the last boy in the game,
so now it's on me to pass the family name.
My folks wish for me to take a wife
but I've already found the love of my life.
Although I was torn, somehow, in the end,
I . . . I found myself leaving him.

He placed the scarf around his neck. He expected her to be angry with him—for attempting to drag her into his lies. He expected her to tell the others, to announce his deception and desert him forever.

Instead, she let out a noise that bellowed across the ship. It echoed as the sails rustled their leaves and the earth beneath them tremored. The sound was so foreign coming from her that it took moments before August registered it was a laugh.

WINNIE.
Of all the women you could've possibly tried,
you chose one who would make the worst bride!

August couldn't remember the last time he felt relief. The leaves became still again.

AUGUST.
Not to mention how horrible I am at fibbing.
I don't know who I thought I was kidding.
I suppose it's my fate to disappoint my kin.

They grew quiet as reality returned, settling around them.

AUGUST.
Now, I've gone and shamed Soloman.
I acted harshly regarding Camelle.

WINNIE.
Does that girl have everyone under a spell?

AUGUST.
Don't start that again. She's kind.
I reckon you'll change your mind.
She even tried to get us together.

WINNIE.
Ha! Did you tell her?

AUGUST.
Haven't found the right moment.
She's been a little heartbroken.

WINNIE.
Those two should get on with it already.
What did she say would charm me?

AUGUST.
She said I needed to be fun.

WINNIE.
You? Fun? *That's* a good one.

AUGUST.
Leo would get a kick out of that.

WINNIE.
Leo, huh? Will you take him back?

AUGUST.
There are other things at stake.
My father has plans for me as of late.
Soon, it'll be my time to run the factory . . .

I'm afraid that I don't have the ability.

WINNIE.
Don't you start! You haven't a thing to fear.
You've been leading us since we got here.
You can run a factory and have a lover.
Who says it must be one or the other?

AUGUST.
What about what my family needs me to do?

WINNIE.
August . . . there's something I should tell you.

Before Winnie could continue, August's face
changed color and his body swayed.
He hit the ground.

*　*　*

In truth, August had been haunted by an evening that
occurred weeks before Reed's death. The entire Norwood
house was asleep, and he had woken in the middle of the
night to get a glass of water.

When he passed by Reed's room, he noticed the
door open and the bed empty. He assumed his brother was
spending the night with a girl, but as he made his way to the
kitchen, he saw light from beneath the door of his father's
study.

August crept toward it, keeping his back against the
wall. He could hear the whispers of both his father and
brother inside, discussing something he did not understand.

His father accused Reed of being foolish. There was no reason to ruin their name over something with no real proof, he explained tersely, especially something that happened years ago. His brother only agreed to keep his mouth shut under certain conditions.

> *"We need better eyes on the factory.*
> *Find out who's to take responsibility.*
> *Someone should watch the assembly line.*
> *We can't let this happen a second time."*

August had no idea what they were referring to. He listened as his father assured Reed that they would take better caution. Why cause a fuss over one faulty match? Their father offered to buy Reed whatever he wanted in return for his silence. Perhaps that motorbike he'd had his eye on? There was a pause before Reed answered.

> *"You'll get one for August, too, then.*
> *Still, that doesn't feel quite even.*
> *Let him leave the family for Leo.*
> *Then we can call it a deal."*

That's when his father began to chuckle, the kind that had frightened them since they were children. He had raised Reed well, he remarked. *"Like father, like son."*

August heard someone move toward the door before it swung open. He slid around the corner and peered behind the wall.

Reed stormed out of the study and through the kitchen to the back door. August had the urge to run after him, but the light from his father's study kept his feet nailed where he stood. He heard a garden statue shatter upon the driveway just before the rumble of his brother's truck faded into the distance.

* * *

CAMELLE.
Soloman. Do you feel the ship moving?

Soloman turned in his cot, the mattress soaked from his perspiration. Eyes closed and body trembling, he responded with a mumble.

SOLOMAN.
That's what it should be doing.

Camelle rose from her cot, the mattress holding her shape like a patch of grass beneath her.

CAMELLE.
I meant that it isn't moving anymore!

Soloman rubbed his eyes and sat up.

SOLOMAN.
Perhaps August had a snore?

Camelle looked across the room.

CAMELLE.
Winnie isn't in her bed.

SOLOMAN.
Ah, so he's found someone to wed.

CAMELLE.
I'm serious. Something's wrong.
Get up and put a shirt on!

Soloman turned his back to her as he dressed, hands
trembling. They stumbled onto the deck. August was
sprawled on the ground as Winnie tried shaking him awake.

WINNIE.
Lend a hand! To the blanket!

Soloman lifted August from beneath his arms as
Winnie grabbed his legs. They laid him down.

SOLOMAN.
Should we try to wake him?

CAMELLE.
He's worn himself thin.
Has he slept or eaten?

Soloman provided a few gentle slaps.

SOLOMAN.
Come on, grouch! Open your eyes!

August's lids trembled as they opened.

AUGUST.
Wh—where am I?
. . . Reed? Is that you?

SOLOMAN.
Whom is he referring to?

August sat up, wincing at the pain.

CAMELLE.
You've had a fall and hit your head.
Perhaps it's time you get some rest.

AUGUST.
I merely fainted. It happens all the time.

SOLOMAN.
You do know recurrence isn't a good sign?

CAMELLE.
Let's wait a few days to see how you feel.
For now, I think Winnie should take the wheel.

* * *

"Leo, please understand. I must find a wife."

"August, you're an adult. This is your life.
We are all blessed with a certain amount of days.
You're going to spend yours doing what they say?"

"Nothing is as dense as blood."

"Nothing is as deep as love!"

"I'm all they've got left now.
It's my duty to make them proud.
You'll always be a part of me,
the rhythm of my melody.
My world was more in tune with you in it."

"Just promise me you'll find the squid."

"Leo, please. It doesn't exist."

"Promise me, August."

* * *

Winnie kept silent as Soloman retrieved a bucket of warm water. She watched Camelle wring a towel and dab August's brow. As she gazed at the man sitting upon the blanket, she thought he looked just like the one she knew, though more absent and somber.

They locked eyes. She would have to wait to tell him. He didn't know it yet, but they were bound. He was a part of her, and she, of him. She moved across the deck, brown leaves crackling like fire beneath her feet. Her hands came out of her coat.

Winnie took the wheel.

The thing about the squid was that no one could determine the exact moment they had learned about it. The awareness of it came about gradually. It greeted them in stages as they grew into adulthood . . . sometimes faintly, other times intensely. The squid survived through rumors spread in hushed voices—theories and thirsts of what it would provide. People agreed on its existence from nothing but a deep longing for it to be real.

Part III:
Winnie

Winnie was winter. Everyone and everything begged her for something whenever she looked at them. They would become desperate for a response from her that would validate their existence. When she glanced at birds, they would cry, *"Look how I fly. Look how my wings flap so gracefully."* When she stepped on the ground, it would shout, *"Look how strong I am! I can hold all of the world's weight!"* When she scraped her knee, it would beg her to wince, to press her palms against it and cry.

She knew they begged her, but she could not offer her attention. She tried, but she could not, for she was numb to everything cruel and everything wonderful.

Winnie never got to kiss happiness. Happiness only gave her flashes of warmth, offered itself to her with no expectations. She wanted to slow its moments, to savor it for more than an instant, but it took her hand, and they ran through what she knew as life. Oh, how they ran. There was not a moment she could taste it, show how much it meant to her, hold it close so it would know for sure. Happiness was too afraid of the wolf chasing them; it never turned around. She wanted to tell it to stop.

"Let it catch us," she would have said. *"Let it swallow us whole."*

It would have been worth one kiss.

* * *

WINNIE.
Will you be all right?

AUGUST.
Don't be silly. I'll be fine.

Winnie examined August's veined hands, the sides of his mouth that curled downwards, the way he shivered as snow drifted on him.

CAMELLE.
It's getting colder on the deck.
Perhaps we should get you to bed.

AUGUST.
Someone give me a hand.
I'm going to try to stand.

Soloman and Camelle helped August up and escorted him downstairs. When they were gone, Winnie weaved through the ship's forest to where she had hidden the pile, in a hole beneath a bare tree. She dug her hand into the slush and pulled an apple from the hoard. Then she slipped it into her pocket and made it back to the wheel.

Soloman appeared through the dark, lit only by the moonlight. Two mugs occupied his hands, the steam rising from them like smoke from a memory.

SOLOMAN.
I'm glad I caught you alone.

WINNIE.
I can't quite read your tone.

SOLOMAN.
I simply wish to talk.
Now, don't look so shocked.
Am I really that bad?

He extended a mug. She took it, the woody notes of coffee greeting her nose.

WINNIE.
Just a tad.

Winnie hadn't figured out how she felt about Soloman. On one hand, she quite liked how he never took things seriously. On the other, she wondered if it was all affectation, a form of manipulation.

SOLOMAN.
I appreciate when others are blunt.
Although, with you, it's just a front.

WINNIE.
I beg your pardon?

SOLOMAN.
Your heart, once soft, has hardened.
Correct me if I'm wrong,
but you weren't always this strong.

Winnie lowered her mug.

WINNIE.
I don't see how that's any business of yours.

SOLOMAN.
I'm not aiming to start a war.
As a matter of fact, I admire you greatly.
I've been wishing for strength myself lately.

WINNIE.
Is that so?

SOLOMAN.
Oh, you know.
Everyone seems to have a mission.
Then there's me, with no ambition.
I pretend that I'm not displeased
witnessing others chase their dreams.
Truth is, I wish I knew what I was after.
So, I disguise my troubles with laughter.

WINNIE.
I thought you were to be a captain.

Wouldn't that be your ambition?

SOLOMAN.
Unfortunately, I wasn't made for it.

WINNIE.
Why are you telling me this?

SOLOMAN.
Because you wouldn't tell anyone else.
You hardly even speak of yourself.

* * *

They had pushed her out the door when she was eighteen with no more than a knapsack of clothes. Although she had watched it happen to the many strays before her, she never thought to plan what she would do when her time came. They had rarely been allowed to go outside, other than to the field out back. Now, she stood staring at endless roads, twisting, and leading to the unknown.

She first stumbled upon a cafe and took a half-eaten tart from an abandoned plate upon a table out front. Then a charming white bridge caught her eye, and she marveled at the way the sunlight made the water glimmer. She crossed the bridge into a park, passing a phone booth beside an enclosed area where dogs played. The area reminded her of the place she hoped never to return, so she passed by without looking in its direction again.

A man hollered at her, whistling between his teeth. She covered her chest with her coat and sprinted as quickly as she could, not caring where her body took her. As the wind hit her cheeks, she felt inhuman—like an animal plunging through a forest. She only stopped when she could no longer breathe, crouching over with hands on her knees.

When she finally looked up, her new home announced its presence so graciously, she felt it too good to be true. She was greeted by brick walls that called her name, engulfed by trees and accompanied by stone walkways. People her age lay in the courtyard, conversing and reading and tasting each other's tongues. It was the most glorious haven she had ever seen. Was this where they all went after the shelter? Or was this a miraculous sanctuary created just for her?

Winnie observed a building with towering white pillars in front. She clutched the straps of her knapsack, climbed the mountain of steps, and entered.

* * *

SOLOMAN.
We're not much different, you and I.
You have that same look in your eyes.
Things don't come to you easy, do they?

WINNIE.
I find a way.

SOLOMAN.
How? How does one beat this curse?

WINNIE.
Simple. Expect the worst.

SOLOMAN.
Another six moons with August?
Well, at least now it's expected.

A puff exited Winnie's lips.

SOLOMAN.
Hold on. Was that a chuckle?

WINNIE.
Yes, but don't feed your ego.

There was something in their banter that reminded
Winnie very much of her conversations with someone else.
She realized then it was the familiarity that made her
cautious.

SOLOMAN.
I won't tell the other two.

He raised his mug.

SOLOMAN.
It was a pleasure talking to you.
Thank you for lending an ear.
Let me know if you need me to steer.

WINNIE.
You? Who never moved our ship?

SOLOMAN.
At least I didn't faint like August.

While we're talking, there's one more thing.
The man's been tracking our supply on this sheet
and is quite sure there's a stockpile missing.
Now, I don't normally listen to his blabbering,
but I must admit, the disparity is staggering.
Do you have an idea where the errors were made?

Winnie saw a gleam in his eyes as he pulled the
paper from his pocket.

WINNIE.
Numbers are not my strength, I'm afraid.

Soloman shrugged and crumpled up the paper.
Winnie noticed how he struggled to keep his mug still.
Though his hands were chapped, she knew the quivers were
not from the cold. She took the coffee from him.

WINNIE.
Drinking this will only make things harder.
Go downstairs and get yourself some water.

SOLOMAN.
Well, then. I'll retreat if I must.
Steer safely. Don't kill us.

He tossed the wad of paper overboard before
disappearing through the trees.

* * *

When Winnie entered the building through the
towering white columns, she had never seen that amount of

reading matter in one place before. The only books she'd read were during their studies at the shelter, always educational texts, never any fiction.

As she browsed the shelves, she stumbled upon a peeling leather chair nestled in the corner of the poetry section. The chair, being against the corner where two walls met, provided a gap just wide enough for Winnie to hide behind, which she did every night at closing. She would stay hidden for about an hour while the custodian swept the floors, who always whistled the same melancholy tune.

When the room was dark and she heard the click of the door locking, she would climb into the chair and read until she grew tired. Then she would brush her teeth and bathe herself with a rag in the washroom. Finally, she'd fall asleep on the floor by the chair until dawn kissed her through the curtains and she snuck out the window before the librarian arrived.

During the day, she sat listening outside open windows of lecture halls where she'd learn Latin and Shakespeare. It was easy for her to roam the university grounds; no one could tell her knapsack was filled with a change of clothes instead of textbooks. For food, she would wait for the students to toss out their lunches, then scour the garbage cans when they wandered off to class. Only once did a student try to speak to her, one who claimed he'd noticed her around but hadn't seen her in any classes, to which she responded that she was the niece of one of the office secretaries and swiftly walked away.

Sometimes she wandered throughout the town, stealing fruit from vendors or taking silverware from tables outside restaurants. She stayed near places where it was crowded, and a few rather threatening incidents taught her to always return to the library before dark. Occasionally, she'd lose track of time and have to keep one hand wrapped tightly around a fork in her pocket as she hurried back to her refuge.

Winnie eventually figured she couldn't keep living that way, deciding it was time to find work somewhere. So, one morning, she snuck out the window just before the librarian arrived, only to walk back through the door and ask if they were hiring.

The librarian, who was a blubbering elderly gentleman with a bad cold, asked about her experience. Having memorized the shelves, Winnie proceeded to tell him where each section was, and how she used to assist her mother who worked at a church's library. This was a lie, of course, which the red-nosed man seemed to be wary of. He began to ask Winnie questions about various things she did not know, such as which novel was so-and-so's third piece of work, or what texts one would recommend to a student of botany.

When she couldn't provide the answers, he sneezed into his handkerchief and told her there weren't any openings.

* * *

CAMELLE.
Men are children when they're ill, aren't they?

Winnie sighed as Camelle approached her. The last thing she wanted at the moment was trivial conversation.

CAMELLE.
August is stubborn, but he'll be okay.

Camelle shivered and rubbed her arms. She spotted
an apple core by Winnie's feet.

CAMELLE.
Are there apple trees on board?
That's strange. I could have sworn . . .

Winnie kept her hands on the wheel as she
continued staring straight ahead.

WINNIE.
I certainly picked baskets full of them.
You must have been busy staring at Soloman.

CAMELLE.
Listen, I wanted to speak with you,
away from the antics of the other two.
I know you don't think me very bright,
but you should know that I'm a midwife.

The word was like an icicle to Winnie's chest.

WINNIE.
What does that have to do with me?

CAMELLE.
You don't have to hide it, Winnie.
I can tell by looking at your face
that you've got a baby on the way.

There's no ring on your finger shown,
so you must be dealing with this all alone.

Camelle's forwardness turned Winnie's body frigid.
She gripped the wheel, her knuckles turning white.

WINNIE.
And you think you could help me?
People like you are the last thing I need.
A few kind words won't solve my problems.

CAMELLE.
Winnie, I'm not trying to solve them.
But there's no use in trying to pretend
that we don't all need a friend.

WINNIE.
Look, I don't know where you're from,
but I suggest you run.
There are wolves in my land
and you . . . you are a lamb.

*   *   *

From the ages of eight to eleven, Winnie had a dear
friend at the shelter named Farah whom she loved more
than anything. She adored Farah's billowy strawberry locks
that grew longer than Winnie's brittle strands ever could.
Winnie found delight in how they bounced whenever Farah
ran toward her with gossip to share, or when she jumped
with glee at the sight of wild rabbits that slipped into the
garden. Farah would do things like share her serving of

porridge on days when Winnie was especially hungry or slip into bed with her when Winnie was cold.

Farah taught Winnie nearly everything she knew—how vast the world was and all its complexities. Farah couldn't even glance at a leaf without having a hundred things to say about it. She'd remark on its intricate skeleton, how its skin faded from green to yellow, and the way it fought against the rain. She'd throw cakes of snow over at the boys' shelter on the other side of the fence, and they would laugh and toss back ones twice as large. She had a way about her that made Winnie love things, and most importantly, she made Winnie love herself.

As they got older, Farah started giving just as much attention to the other girls. Winnie tried not to let it bother her. What kind of person would she be, after all, to want someone reserved only for her? That would have been as silly as it was selfish.

Farah proved to be quite attentive, for one evening, when they were washing their faces before bed, she turned to Winnie and said:

"Don't make anything of it.
You'll always be my favorite."

Then she turned off the tap and skipped out of the washroom.

Winnie felt better for a while after that. Then one morning, they finished their breakfast to find a couple—the wife politely clutching a fancy handbag with both hands, the husband holding his arm around her shoulders—standing in the center of the recreation room. The couple introduced themselves as Mr. and Mrs. Upton.

The other girls immediately began to fix their hair and straighten their skirts before pretending to knit or sew like good girls were to do. Winnie, who thought the charade ridiculous, continued to hammer at the birdhouse that she and Farah had been constructing for weeks.

This time, however, Farah ignored her request for assistance on the roof. Instead, she walked right up to Mr. and Mrs. Upton and curtseyed. The couple seemed to take a liking to Farah, and after about an hour of them following her around the shelter, and another hour inside the matrons' office, it was announced that Farah was being adopted.

After Farah left, Winnie never did make another friend at the shelter.

* * *

CAMELLE.
If that is truly how you feel,
then I'll leave you to the wheel.

A brown bundle of blankets waddled onto the deck.

CAMELLE.
August! You should be in bed.

AUGUST.
I thought I'd get fresh air instead.
Mother of pearl spit. It's freezing.

CAMELLE.
I'm sorry. If you'll excuse me.

Camelle pushed by him and faded into the mist.
August turned to Winnie.

AUGUST.
What'd you do this time?

WINNIE.
My business is mine.
Why do people find that hard to accept?

AUGUST.
They're only trying to connect.

WINNIE.
No one really wants to know who I am.
They pretend to, but it's all a sham.
I'm never what they end up seeking.
Broken shells are not worth keeping.

AUGUST.
Right. I see. It's a form of control,
why you act so cold.

WINNIE.
I may be cold, but at least one knows what to expect.
I'm tired of kindness one day, disloyalty the next.
People take their own words and toss them away.
They no longer matter if they were said yesterday.

AUGUST.
You'll only hurt yourself if you retaliate.
Don't become part of the world you hate.

August tightened the blankets that cloaked him and blew what warmth he had into his hands. Winnie watched him shuffle back downstairs. The earthiness of his presence lingered long after he left, a scent reminiscent of cinnamon and clove.

* * *

The idea of belonging to someone never did make sense to Winnie. No one belonged to anyone, only themselves. And yet, there was a loneliness that haunted her, a curiosity as to what it would feel like. She never belonged to a mother or father, and she sure didn't belong to the matrons at the shelter. She would have liked to belong to Farah . . . but Farah evidently preferred belonging to Mr. and Mrs. Upton.

It wasn't that Winnie needed to belong to anyone per se. It just would have been nice to know that someone would miss her if she were gone.

* * *

Camelle moved with a furrowed brow through the deck, which was now a pale-blue canvas with tree trunks painted black. She was surprised to find Soloman at the stern.

CAMELLE.
It's a wonder how you never get cold.

SOLOMAN.
There's something about the sunrise through snow.

They watched light arc through silver clouds as the moon shared a sky with the sun. Flakes swirled around them, glowing like fireflies.

SOLOMAN.
Camelle . . . I don't want to fight.

CAMELLE.
I know. I fear that you were right.
Perhaps I'm nothing but naive.
I'm a lamb in a world of beasts.
Why have goodness when no one cares?
One might as well conform to a world unfair.

SOLOMAN.
It's normal to feel a little unsure,
but don't forget what you said before.
You don't care what others are like,
only who you are in this life.
Look at you, Elle. You offer so much.
Me, however? I'm just a crutch.
People lean on me when they despise their lives.
We drink and dance and it's fun 'til sunrise.
Then they wake, regretful and daunted,
while I discover the feeling of being unwanted.

He took another glance at the sun, its rays now highlighting the bends and twists of every tree branch.

SOLOMAN.
Don't you dare think you must go conforming.
You're the one they'll still want in the morning.

Camelle peered through the gaps of the forest. She could see the distant shape of Winnie teetering the wheel, as though unsure of where to go.

*   *   *

Winnie's least yet most favorite day was Sunday when the library would remain closed. While this meant she could sleep in and read all the books she wanted throughout the day, it also gave her a lot of time to be in her thoughts—which often made it difficult to want to do anything at all.

Some Sundays she would lay on the floor, curled up to the side, using her coat as a blanket, staring at whatever books were on the bottom shelves. Her eyes would move down the line, skimming each title as she tried to decide which to read, but her mind would not be able to find one that felt like it would satisfy her.

She'd try willing her body to move, but it would not. She'd even try breaking the action into steps: *Lift your head, sit up, stand, grab a book . . .* No matter how many times she repeated the steps, she'd find herself remaining on the floor for another few hours. She would be so unwilling to move that she would not even bother to search for food; it was only when the commode beckoned that she would finally get up.

*   *   *

The shrouded sun rose and set two dozen times as ice glazed the deck. With each passing day, the four struggled even more to keep from slipping, their steps turning the floor black.

One such afternoon, Winnie observed from the wheel as Soloman crossed the ship with both his arms outstretched. Meanwhile, August held on to a vine, only to realize his hand had become stuck to it.

AUGUST.
Mother of pearl spit!

Camelle slid toward him and released the warmth of her breath onto his hand. August let out a yelp as she ripped the vine from it.

WINNIE.
It's like watching a circus.

SOLOMAN.
I'm risking my life with every step.

CAMELLE.
Perhaps we should stay below deck.

WINNIE.
Relax. Dig inside that tree trunk.

Camelle glided to the hollow tree and, one by one, pulled out eight sharp staffs.

CAMELLE.
These are for us?

SOLOMAN.
Look at that. She does have a heart.

WINNIE.
Just trying to do my part.
There's no need for you fools to fall.

SOLOMAN.
So she wasn't trying to kill us after all.

They each dug two staffs into the slush, marching
with confidence on their new slender limbs. Winnie kept
hers by the wheel. She would need them to grab fruit while
the others slept.

AUGUST.
Brilliant. I can walk the deck all day!

CAMELLE.
Not so fast. What did I say?
You must rest if you're to get stronger.

AUGUST.
Fine, fine. I'll stay out just a bit longer.
Oh no, there's muck on my shoes.
I may have spoken too soon . . .

Camelle left a muttering August and treaded toward
the wheel. The frost nipped at her cheeks as she approached
Winnie. They stood for a moment, taking in the quiet
twirling flakes.

CAMELLE.
If your contractions are far apart,
then they are merely false alarms.

And if you have trouble breathing,
stand up tall and that will ease it.

Winnie turned toward the sea. Though she didn't care for Camelle's kindness, she had to respect her stubbornness. And if Winnie were being honest, she had no idea what to do about the life inside her. There were times where even the slightest bit of discomfort made her panic. It would have been nice to have someone tell her what was normal.

She turned to Camelle and gave a nod that eased them both.

They looked at the other two. One was compulsively shaking slush off his shoes with every step. The other had discovered he could pitch his staffs into the ground and swing himself between them.

CAMELLE.
You can't hide this for long.
You'll need to tell August and Soloman.
Why did you keep this from us?

WINNIE.
I almost told August.

CAMELLE.
It's not his, is it?

WINNIE.
Don't be ridiculous.

CAMELLE.
Well, your secret is safe with me,
including the stash beneath that tree.

WINNIE.
Wh—How did you see them?

CAMELLE.
A protruding stem.

Winnie cursed herself for having hid the fruit in the
same place she'd kept the staffs.

WINNIE.
For the baby . . . I must keep feeding—

CAMELLE.
I know. I'll bring you stew when they're sleeping.

Although Camelle walked away with her head held
high, Winnie swore she heard sniffling against the rhythm of
staffs piercing the ice.

* * *

One Sunday, Winnie was buried so deep, her coat
was covered up to her nose. The weather had been warm for
a while, but she'd chosen to be hidden over comfort.
She had been on the floor for nearly twelve hours
when she heard voices outside the library door. She bolted
up, bunched her coat and knapsack in her arms, and slid a
window open. As the lock turned, she tossed out her things,

hoisted herself onto the sill, and slipped through the opening. Then she left the window cracked so as to not make noise.

Her eyes adjusted to the brightness as she heard a man's voice inside.

"Now, it is usually cleaner than this, but our custodian doesn't get in until the evening. It's also not normally this stuffy . . ."

Winnie listened as the man rambled on about how much the students loved spending time there and how the library's selection housed the latest editions of all the textbooks. She heard the voices of a couple asking him questions, such as what hours the students were allowed to access the library, and what would happen if the text they needed had been checked out.

"I can assure you, we have enough editions," the man answered. *"Allow me to show you . . ."*

Winnie could hear them getting closer to her window, so she stayed crouched against the wall and moved around the building, dragging her things with her. When she got to the other side, she put on her knapsack, eyeing her escape. If she stood up behind the wall and walked past the line of windows, she would appear to be someone casually strolling by. She decided to take that path.

Folding her coat over her arm, she stood and coolly marched forward. All seemed to be going well until she felt a presence at the last window. She turned.

There stood a grown Farah, adorned in pearls, staring at her through the glass in a daze.

Winnie, Farah mouthed, before sprinting for the door.

The next few minutes were a blur. Winnie felt arms fling themselves around her. Farah's once billowy locks were now cut short, curls bouncing by her ears. Winnie suddenly became very self-conscious, cursing herself for not having bathed that morning.

Farah chatted away, asking Winnie questions without offering any pause for answers. What was she doing here? Who had taken her in? Where did she live now?

Now that Farah was of age, Mr. and Mrs. Upton were taking her on a private tour of the university. They felt she had the aptitude to become an architect.

"Imagine! Me . . . designing at a real job.
I suppose all those birdhouses paid off."

At this point, Mr. and Mrs. Upton came outside with a stout mustached man behind them, still blubbering about the various things the university offered.

Farah told them that Winnie was an old friend. They greeted her kindly and suggested she come over for Farah's birthday party the following week.

And though Winnie's mind told her to decline, she found herself agreeing, nevertheless.

* * *

AUGUST.
How is Winnie doing?

CAMELLE.
Well, the ship's moving.

She made the beds around them as she spoke,
fluffing pillows and straightening out tangled blankets.

AUGUST.
Good. She's a capable one.

CAMELLE.
Have you found your . . . "fun"?

AUGUST.
Why are you saying it so strangely?
No, I've had other things on my mind lately.

CAMELLE.
You haven't spent time with her at all?

August sat up, groaning and clutching his back.

AUGUST.
Hardly. Is something going on?

CAMELLE.
No, I simply wondered.

AUGUST.
You're sneaky. Like my brother.

Camelle frowned at the flatness of Winnie's pillow.
She hit it a few times around the sides, but it refused to
plump up.

CAMELLE.
How many siblings have you got?

AUGUST.
Just the one. But uh— He's gone.
Actually. . . we were twins.

Camelle set down the pillow.

CAMELLE.
Oh, August. How long has it been?

AUGUST.
A little over six months.

CAMELLE.
And I told you to be fun!
I'm so desperately sorry.

AUGUST.
Ah, not to worry.

Camelle twisted her hands, searching for words.

CAMELLE.
How is your head now?

AUGUST.
Loads better, somehow.
I could have been worse.
You must be a nurse.

CAMELLE.
Something like that.

AUGUST.
Do you know where Soloman's at?

CAMELLE.
For once, I do.
Did he do something to you?

AUGUST.
Not at all.
Matter of fact, it was my fault.
I fear I've said harsh words.

CAMELLE.
I'm sure that they were deserved.

A chill ran through the room. Camelle took a
blanket from her own cot and placed it over August's lap.

CAMELLE.
Perhaps I should make some tea.
Do you take yours with honey?
I can barely think in this cold!

AUGUST.
There's no need. Please don't go.

Camelle tilted her head when she heard his tone.
She sat at the edge of August's cot by his side. The mattress
sunk beneath her like a mound of leaves.

AUGUST.
Listen, regarding Winnie and I . . .
I appreciated your kind advice.
However, I've been dishonest
and think it's time I confess.
It's true my folks wish me a wife,
but there's already a love in my life.

He looked down, gently tugging at a loose thread
from a blanket.

AUGUST.
I'm aiming to do what they asked.
Winnie's trying to keep me from that.

CAMELLE.
I . . . I don't understand.
Why not take your love's hand
and make her your wife?

August laughed for the first time in a while.

AUGUST.
He couldn't be a wife if he tried.

CAMELLE.
Oh! I can't believe I've acted so cruel.
Once again, I've been a fool.

AUGUST.
Nonsense. You didn't know.
And see, the thing with my folks . . .

They wish for me to have a son.

CAMELLE.
I must side with Winnie on this one.

AUGUST.
I never thought I'd live to see
the day the two of you would agree.

CAMELLE.
How long have you loved him for?

AUGUST.
Right. That, I can't be sure—

CAMELLE.
August.

AUGUST.
Six.

CAMELLE.
Six, what?
Months?

AUGUST.
Years.

CAMELLE.
Oh, dear.

The thread unraveled, producing a hole in the
blanket. Camelle pried it from August's rigid fingers.

CAMELLE.
Listen. I know what it's like to be haunted by someone.
Nothing compares to the love had when we were young.
If you're lucky enough to hold on to it, you should.
Usually, I wouldn't change the past if I could,
but we all have a time when we wish we'd done more.
Promise you won't let this one become yours.

*　*　*

Farah lived in a building fancy enough to have a
doorman. Unlike most flats that shared walls with other
buildings, this one stood on its own, four stories high and
two balconies wide.

When Winnie got there, the first thing she noticed
were the leafy vines that crawled up the front walls. Though
they were vines, they were neatly trimmed, purposeful and
self-assured.

Farah greeted her on the first floor, offering an
embrace just as warm as before. She led Winnie to the
stairwell, prattling about her friends from secondary school
who were there.

Winnie eventually managed to interject Farah's
chatter.

*"I wondered about your party's date,
given that we don't know our birthdays."*

"Oh! We say it's a birthday, but you know,

it's really the day they brought me home."

"Of course. How could I forget?"

Farah ignored her response. She stopped at the bottom of the staircase and smoothed Winnie's hair, her fingers moving slowly and delicately.

"There we go. Now you're all set.
Listen, my friends don't know my past,
so best not mention the shelter if they ask.
Let's just say you're a visiting cousin."

With every flight of stairs that they climbed, Winnie dreaded the visit more and more. Her chest throbbed along with her thighs, and she wished she could slide down the rails and vanish into the lobby floor.

Eventually, they reached the very top. Farah led her to one of two doors and put her hand on the knob.

"Mum and Dad are staying at a hotel,
so we've got the place to ourselves."

Winnie was thrown by hearing those words used for Mr. and Mrs. Upton, but she supposed it only made sense.

When they got inside, Winnie immediately felt out of place. Everything was spotless. The furniture appeared more for display than something one lived with, color-coordinated with its lavenders and blues and violets. Regardless, there sat eight girls on velvet couches, laughing and playing blackjack while jazz echoed throughout the rooms.

Across from them, a dining table was covered in accessories, boxes of taffy, and baskets with giant bows. Farah noticed Winnie staring at the table in awe.

"These are for everyone to take home.
Be sure to grab some before you go!
Here, why don't you wear this hat?"

"Oh, I . . . I don't really need that."

"Come on! It's just for fun!
Let me introduce you to everyone."

Farah placed an ostrich feather hat on Winnie's head and pushed her down in a bergère. Winnie did her best to play along with their games, but for the most part, she remained quiet. The girls babbled on about their plans after graduation and giggled over the teachers they found attractive. Finally, someone suggested they cut the cake.

One of the girls pushed a candle in the center of the pink frosting as another rummaged through the kitchen drawers.

"Farah, have you got any matches?
You can't have cake without a wish!"

Winnie realized her escape and spoke for the first time since the evening began.

"I'll go out and get a box."

The girls looked at her. She cleared her throat.

"I . . . I could use a walk."

So, Farah handed her some change, and Winnie shuffled out the door. She took her time, ambling along paths beside railroad tracks that cut through the town.

At the corner store, she refrained from looking at the shelves of boxed biscuits that could keep her full for days. There were numerous assorted matchboxes at the register, and as she fumbled through them, Winnie noticed the clerk staring at her. She'd almost forgotten that she was still wearing that ridiculous hat. How strange it must have appeared for such an extravagant item to be worn with a frayed coat.

Winnie found a matchbox that caught her eye. The front displayed the silhouettes of trees, placed together to form the shape of a house. It reminded her of the birdhouses she and Farah used to build, so she slid the change across the counter and slipped the box into her pocket.

When she arrived back at the flat, the others must not have heard her, for they spoke about her as she stood right there in the doorway.

"Your cousin is strange, isn't she?
Has she not learned to speak?"

"She's shy is all. I feel for her.
She's my dead uncle's daughter
and has no one left but me.
Poor little Winnie . . .
Her clothes aren't quite the right size,
but she has no mother to teach her otherw—"

Farah stopped when she saw Winnie. The others went silent.

After a moment, Farah turned off the record player and thanked everyone for coming. She told them how grateful she was for their gifts and how she hoped they would visit again soon. She admitted that she was quite tired from the festivities and ought to get some rest. The girls all stood from their seats, avoided looking at Winnie, and gave Farah kisses on each cheek, who made sure that they departed with souvenirs and a slice of peppermint cake for the road.

As soon as they were gone, Winnie scoffed.

"Don't pretend like you care for me.
I see I'm just an act of charity.
Do you feel like a good human being,
helping your 'poor little Winnie'?"

"I offered you more than you can carry.
Couldn't you have at least tried acting merry?"

Winnie ripped the hat from her head and threw it at Farah.

"Keep your things. I don't want them.
I knew I shouldn't have come."

Farah furiously straightened out the feathers.

"You've completely ruined my day!"

"Did I? Let's fix that with some cake."

Winnie pulled the box from her pocket, struck a match against it, and lit the lonely candle embedded in the remaining slice.

"Be sure to make a wish!
Just don't tell me what it is.
Though it's lavish, I'm sure."

"Oh, that's very mature!"

Winnie went out to the balcony as Farah continued yelling. The evening air had grown cooler since she'd arrived. She gazed out at the view of the town. Beyond it, the ocean glistened beneath the moonlight. She had never seen it from above before. It both amazed and angered her.

Farah followed her, demanding a response. Winnie spotted the pillars of the library, now small and unremarkable. Her eyes remained glued to the miniature white columns as she finally acknowledged Farah's outburst.

"It's absurd, what you've become."

"This is what all of us dreamed of.
You can't be upset now that I've got it.
Otherwise, you're just a hypocrite!"

"Did you think of me even once after you left?
Or did all your pretty bows help you forget?"

"What did you want me to do? Give it up?
I'm sharing it now—isn't that enough?"

"I don't understand what you want from me!"

"I know you don't attend the university."

Winnie faced Farah. The girl she once knew was still behind the powder caked upon her face. She examined her lips, recalling how they had once been covered in porridge, or banana pudding if they were lucky. And as she stared at the red paint that coated them now, what they said next stirred the squall within her.

"Winnie, I only want to help you."

"Well, I don't want you to!"

The air was no longer cool. Winnie noticed a flickering at the corner of her eye.

They both turned to the room. The dining table was ablaze, along with the gifts upon it. Flames engulfed the wall it touched, spreading across the carpet.

Farah screamed as she ran into the flat, attempting to put it out with water from various flower vases.

"Farah!" Winnie urged. *"We're on the top floor. Get to the door!"*

Farah refused. *"My things!"* she cried. *"My hats, my shoes, my rings!"*

Winnie dragged her out as she fought, flames chasing them like beasts hunting their prey. She forced Farah through the haze and shoved her out of the flat. Farah sobbed through her coughs as Winnie pulled her down the stairs. Other residents flew out of their doors, bodies colliding as they descended.

One flight, two flights, three flights, four.

When they got outside, Winnie tried to console her, but Farah shoved her away.

"Don't you see?
They will never forgive me!
Watching the place was all I had to do,
and now it's gone because of you!"

"I'm sorry, I don't know what happened!"

"I never want to see you again!"

Farah ran from her. Sirens blared in the distance, drowning out the crackle of the blaze as they grew closer.

Winnie watched as the building's leafy vines curled like tormented worms. She looked up, ashes snowing violently from the sky—a sight that would remain forever in her mind, a constant reminder of her faults. A winter in summer.

* * *

CAMELLE.
Here. Careful, it's hot.

Winnie took the bowl of stew from Camelle.

WINNIE.
We'll get caught.

CAMELLE.
They're both sleeping soundly . . .
and snoring quite loudly.
I'm glad they're finally able to shut their eyes.
They were restless for quite some time.

WINNIE.
You've helped me for two moons.
If we keep on, we'll run out of food.
I'm afraid they'll start to notice.
Perhaps it's time we stop doing this.

CAMELLE.
They haven't noticed your fingers grow
or that giant bump under your coat!
Do you think they'd really see
a few bowls of stew missing?
There's no point stifling your appetite
when the baby's about to arrive.
We'll talk after you get some sleep.
Now, you shouldn't be on your feet.
I don't know why I asked you to steer!

WINNIE.
It's all right. I want to be here.
It helps keep me occupied.

Winnie had very few quiet nights. Sometimes, when
she closed her eyes, she would see the unforgiving flames,
breathe the noxious smoke, feel the angry heat.

CAMELLE.
There's something on your mind.

Winnie fixated on the steam rising from the bowl in her hands.

CAMELLE.
You're scared.
Do you feel unprepared?

Winnie didn't answer.

CAMELLE.
Come, now. What is it?

WINNIE.
What if I'm horrible at this?
Some days, I want this badly.
I feel a kick and I'm . . . happy.
Then I remember the harm I cause
to everyone in my life that ever was.

CAMELLE.
That's not true.

WINNIE.
Look how I treated you.
I'm not easy to be around.
What if I let my own child down?

CAMELLE.
That's a common thing to fear.

WINNIE.
I can't do this without him here.

CAMELLE.
You mean the father?

Winnie began to cry, each tear a different shape upon her cheeks.

CAMELLE.
I'm sorry. You're bothered.
I didn't mean to—

WINNIE.
It's not you.
The father's not—

AUGUST.
What's going on?

August and Soloman appeared on the deck.

AUGUST.
Have you been eating?
That was to be evenly divided!

WINNIE.
I'm sorry! I didn't want to hide it.

AUGUST.
The whole time, it was you? I was sure—

CAMELLE.
It was me. I gave it to her.

Camelle took the bowl from Winnie's trembling hands.

AUGUST.
How could you? We're all hungry!

WINNIE.
August, please don't be angry.

CAMELLE.
Winnie. You should tell them now.

AUGUST
What could be enough to break our vow?

WINNIE.
I admit, I hid one of our piles,
but I did so because . . . I'm with child.
I needed to be sure I'd have enough.

SOLOMAN.
Well, why didn't you just tell us?

WINNIE.
May I have a moment with August?

SOLOMAN.
You're kidding. Don't tell me it's his?

WINNIE.
Why does—no! I'm far along.
It happened before I met you all.

CAMELLE.
Soloman, if you please.
Come, and leave them be.

They retreated downstairs.

Winnie and August stood alone. He was a part of her, and she, of him. The quietness consumed them as he searched her face. Light flakes trickled from an infinite dark sky.

AUGUST.
Right. You're . . . having a baby.
What does that have to do with me?

* * *

Winnie knew she didn't have much time left at the library before Farah would attend school there. Would Farah report her to the university? Would she give her away by telling other students? As much as she wanted to place trust in the friend she once knew, there was no way of knowing who she was now. Winnie needed to find work, and she needed it soon.

She rested on the steps in front of the building, sitting between the towering columns that had been her home. The dew of the morning painted the grass of the courtyard a glistening white.

Winnie slipped her hands into her coat and felt something inside.

She pulled out the matchbox.

As she stared at the logo, it called her name. She turned the box over and read the address printed in petite letters.

It would take half a day's walk, which was plenty of time to think about what to say when she got there. As she trekked across cobblestones and through the park onto the bridge, the morning when she first stepped into the world felt so long ago. She stared at the water, no longer glistening as it had that day. She only stopped to glance, but she could not look away from its stillness. Fearing her wandering mind, she focused on a bird feather floating by as she developed a plan.

She would ask for the boss at the factory, then tell him she had experience processing wood for an old architect. If he asked for a reference, she would give him the number to the payphone in the park and say the retired architect was going out of town the following day—he must be called first thing in the morning. Then when the payphone rang, she would pick up pretending to be the architect's wife and say he had just gone out the door, but she could vouch for Winnie just the same. Winnie was sure the plan would work perfectly as long as she stayed by the payphone all morning.

Yet, when she finally got to the factory building, smoke billowing from the top, Winnie fell to her knees. The matchbox slipped from the numbness of her hands, her doubts overcoming determination. Would there ever be a place where she was wanted?

She felt herself sobbing. She couldn't remember the last time she'd cried, and now, she could not seem to stop. A cluster of loneliness, dread, and despair whirled inside her, taking turns in stealing the breath from her lungs.

"Miss, can I help you with anything at all?
Perhaps some change or someone I could call?"

She attempted to dry her eyes, but the impossibility of it only made her sob more. There was no hiding it. As she stood, her determination returned, and she forged on.

"I . . . I was hoping there'd be work for me."

"I do apologize. It's family only."

"Family only? Who's in charge here?"

"That would be Otto Norwood, miss.
Is there something I can help you with?"

"Well, are you this . . . 'Otto' someone?"

"Apologies. The name's Reed. I'm his son."

* * *

Camelle cleared the bowl of cold stew in the kitchen before hurrying into the other room. Soloman followed her anxiously.

SOLOMAN.
Are you going to tell me?
Is it or is it not his baby?

CAMELLE.
If you would shut up, we'd know!

She glided past the cots and crept to the top of the
stairwell, pointing her ear up to the deck.

SOLOMAN.
So much for leaving them alone.

CAMELLE.
Oh! I can't make out their words!

SOLOMAN.
Perhaps they're not meant to be heard.
The details aren't worth it if we must pry.

CAMELLE.
I despise it when you're right.

She sat down upon the steps. He sat beside her, and
although there was no drink in his hand, he found courage
just the same.

SOLOMAN.
When I was gone and at the academy,
I often wondered what you were doing.
I should have known you'd become a midwife,
that you'd be helping others bring life.

You bring life to everything you touch.

He looked at her, the rays of his eyes dimming.

SOLOMAN.
Elle, I've missed you so much.
I'm sorry for what I did to you.

CAMELLE.
You don't know what you put me through.

A burst of snow whirled into the stairwell, landing
upon them both.

SOLOMAN.
I don't expect you to forgive me,
but you at least deserve an apology.
When I saw the fire, I realized the harm I'd caused.
Your mother always did see through my flaws.
I knew then that what she believed was right.
I was a dangerous flame waiting to ignite.

CAMELLE.
You know what makes this all so funny?
You only proved her right by running.

SOLOMAN.
Irony has always been my greatest tragedy.
If I could go back, I'd do it all differently.

CAMELLE.
I used to think I'd have so much to say.

All those years, I was waiting for this day.
Now, I realize I'm not ready to discuss this.
Let us focus on finding the squid.

SOLOMAN.
You've still got it on your mind?

CAMELLE.
Of course I do. We're running out of time.

SOLOMAN.
Do you think they're still looking for it?

CAMELLE.
Everybody is.

SOLOMAN.
You were right about them . . . before.
They haven't thrown us overboard.

Voices grew louder from the deck. Camelle put a
finger to her lips. They listened.

CAMELLE.
She said, ". . . right . . . before . . . his death."
Why, of course! I should have guessed!

SOLOMAN.
I don't get it. What's been uncovered?

CAMELLE.
You see . . . August had a brother.

* * *

Winnie grew to like Reed. He read even more books than she did and could entertain any analyses she had about what the clouds meant in a certain novel, or how the food reflected each characters' nature. He had a rebuttal for every theory she had, and each time he disagreed with her, she found him more invigorating to be around.

At first they met up around the university, where she told him she was a student. After a while, he would pick her up and they'd take long drives and dine at different establishments outside town. Winnie liked that Reed chose to drive the truck, despite being able to afford fancy cars. She loved climbing in order to get into it, the rumble beneath her, the knocking of lumber in the cargo bed.

The more she spent time with him, the more she found it hard to keep up her lie until one evening at a café, as they finished their apple pie à la mode, she could do it no more. Hot fused with cold as she swallowed a spoonful of crust and ice cream. He sat there, beaming at her, until the words overflowed from her mouth.

"I'm a stray."

His face grew serious as he leaned back in his chair.

She made an effort to memorize the length of his nose, the way his mouth curled downwards, the red bristles across his chin, supposing it would be the last time she would see his features.

He cleared his throat.

"Where do you stay?"

There was no reason to conceal anything now.

She told him about her time at the shelter, how she stumbled upon the campus and found refuge in the library. She admitted her troubles finding work, how there were days she couldn't get out of bed no matter how much she willed it. She described the uneasiness she felt around other people, and how often she wanted to disappear.

"I wish I could live where no one would see me.
A place where I'd blend in with the trees."

"Get in the car. We've got a place to go."

"I need to get back. The library will close."

"You're not going back there.
You won't sleep there again, I swear.
Now take your bag and get in the car."

"I certainly can't stay where you are.
Your family will surely throw a fit."

"Will you just trust me and get in?"

Reed drove through the winding road to his family's estate. When they got there, he got out of the truck to unlock an iron gate, adorned with the letter *N* in its center. The sun had begun its descent, hovering just above the faded ridges and peaks in the distance.

The *N* split apart as Reed pushed open the doors. Winnie ogled at the manor, windows on the first floor still bright with activity. As they zoomed by it, Reed instructed

her to hide her head, and when it was finally safe for her to
sit up, they were roaring through an aspen forest.

Winnie turned to him.

"Are you going to kill me?"

*"I'm the one that should be worried.
Pretty sure you could beat me in a match."*

"So . . . will you tell me where we're at?"

Reed drove up a dirt road, which swirled itself
around a mountain. As they went higher and higher, the
truck groaned louder and louder. The path began to blend
in with the ground.

"Only a little more to get through."

"You're lucky I like you."

The cabin sat in a clearing, crafted by the same trees
that made way for it. Reed lit the lantern hanging out front as
shelter revealed itself within the darkness. He had spent
years constructing it, he told her, for moments when being a
Norwood was too much.

Winnie examined the log structure, about eighteen
by twenty-four. There was no glass in the windows, and the
roof needed work, but it was impressive for something built
by a single person.

"When you're here, where do they think you are?"

"Oh, you know, out spending time with a broad."

"Sooner or later, wouldn't they find this?"

"No. You'll be safe, I promise.
It's too high up the mountain
to haul lumber without sliding.
There's no reason for them to go this way
with plenty of aspens on the estate."

"I can't take this place from you."

"Please. You need it more than I do.
There are parts, though, not yet finished."

"Those can be easily fixed.
I've built some things in my time."

"Why am I not surprised?"

"Reed, I can't thank you enough."

"Ah, there's no need for that stuff.
Anyway, I know privacy is important to you,
so I won't come by unless you want me to.
The place is officially yours to keep."

"Why would you do this for me?"

"No one can survive on their own.
You can't keep spending your life alone.
We all need help from time to time."

"Was that supposed to be a line?"

"Depends on if it worked."

"Not with that smirk."

And with that, Reed dropped his smile as Winnie found hers.

* * *

SOLOMAN.
You're telling me there were two of them?

CAMELLE.
For the love of all things, Soloman,
this isn't that difficult to follow.

SOLOMAN.
It's just a lot to swallow.
I shouldn't have teased August . . .
I couldn't tell you why I did.
I think I envied his sense of duty,
though that's no excuse for cruelty.
And Winnie . . . that poor woman.

CAMELLE.
She's got tough skin.
She'll be a wonderful mother.

SOLOMAN.
How did she meet his brother?

CAMELLE.
I don't know. I couldn't hear.
But I do know that she cared.
We can only hope that a bit of relief
comes from them sharing their grief.

* * *

The cabin was filled with enough books to satisfy Winnie for quite some time. Reed had filled it with every title he'd owned since he was a child, and he also provided every iron tool Winnie could ask for. The collection of hammers, saws, and axes kept her plenty busy. During the day, she would chop wood or build hunting traps, despite Reed's insistence that he could just bring her meals. In the night, she would toss the wood into the furnace and read in the warmth.

Whenever Reed decided to visit, he would call the cabin's telephone and let it ring exactly four times before hanging up. If Winnie wanted him to come over, she was to immediately call back and let it ring exactly two times before hanging up. If she didn't want him to come over, she was to not ring back at all. This system worked well for the most part, except for one time when Reed's uncle happened to pick up the telephone from the other room on Winnie's first ring and she was forced to hang up without saying anything.

Reed rang once every other week or so, and Winnie only wanted a visit from him half the time. This meant the two saw each other about a dozen times per year. Despite that, Winnie received a marriage proposal from Reed at least twice a year.

Winnie knew marriage would not be suitable for the
way she cared for Reed. She wanted him to bathe in his
youth and explore a world outside his family. She wanted
him to laugh until his sides twinged and taste exotic foods
and tongues until he was whole. She wanted him to talk
about his day—where he went and who he spent it with. She
never minded when he came to her smelling of sweat and
perfume. She wasn't hurt by divided attention like she had
been with Farah, and she inwardly wondered if either of
those experiences was love.

* * *

AUGUST.
I find this all hard to believe.
That just doesn't sound like Reed.
Why would he hide you from us all?

WINNIE.
I asked not to be involved.
I was a recluse, and he respected that.
Marriage was never where my mind was at.
I always encouraged him to find someone
and didn't mind him pursuing other women.
The more that were seen around Reed,
the less people cared when he was with me.
We had an understanding, he and I.
One that worked for quite some time.

AUGUST.
I apologize, but I must say this.
You'll have to find a way to prove it.

Half the things about us are in the paper.
How do I know you're not a faker?
We get those every now and then . . .
people pretending to be an uncle's friend.
You could have built a cabin, claimed it Reed's.

WINNIE.
How would I have entered the property?
Or gotten the tools for construction?
August, I never meant for an introduction,
but when you told me your problems,
I realized only I could solve them.
If I'm carrying your brother's son,
I may be the one to save your love.
I'm not certain a boy is what it will be,
but there's a chance you'd be set free!

AUGUST.
Was befriending me all an act?

WINNIE.
No! I would never do that.
When I lost him, I needed to do something with myself,
so I decided to seek the squid like everyone else.
If not for me, then at least for my child.
Anyway, I was on the ship for a while
and eventually, a part of me knew
that you were onboard too.
You see, Reed always talked about his twin.
I figured seeing you would be like . . . seeing him.
When I found you, I tried to keep my distance,
but you Norwoods are incredibly persistent!

AUGUST.
Right. I still don't understand.
None of this makes any sense.
Even if you had no plans to come near,
how did you know that I would be here?

WINNIE.
Because you lost him, too.

Frost lined the remaining leaves of umber. Flakes turned to heavy snow as they faced each other through the blizzard.

WINNIE.
August, I was meant to find you.

The water that hugged the ship began to freeze.

WINNIE.
Our friendship is as real as the sea,
but I understand if you no longer trust me.
I never did go about things the right way.
Reed was the only one in my life who stayed.
He gave me so much more than I deserved.
It should have been me who left this earth.

The vessel convulsed, sounds of cracking ice nearly deafening their ears. They looked up to find glaciers emerging from beneath the ocean.
Soloman and Camelle ran to them, looking as frigid as the trees they tore through.

SOLOMAN.
You can't stay here! It's too risky!

CAMELLE.
Follow us below deck! Quickly!

Winnie took a step before shaking her head. She hung on to the wheel.

WINNIE.
If I fall, the baby will be harmed.

AUGUST.
Then you better hang on to my arm.

*   *   *

Because the cabin was the one place where Reed didn't have to put on a front, that meant Winnie often witnessed the worst sides of him.

At the beginning, he confided in her over steel cups of tea. Eventually, he felt comfortable enough to knock on the door with tears in his eyes. Winnie would never ask what was wrong, and after a while he stopped needing to tell her. He'd merely stumble inside and crawl into bed as she held him.

By the fourth year, he'd burst through the door in a rage. She never challenged him for not having first rang the telephone like he used to. She felt she had no right, for the cabin was his, after all. So, she'd let him throw his tantrums, broken plates here and there, but he never once laid a finger on her. After he cooled down, he would make it up to her by taking her to the circus or an emporium.

By the sixth year, the cabin seemed too small for the both of them. There would be times when Winnie would be unable to leave the bed, and Reed's outbursts made her want to sink into the mattress. Other times, she would be at peace, enjoying the climax of a novel, and the sound of breaking glass would ruin her ability to concentrate. She missed the politeness and respect he once had for her by ringing before coming over. She wanted to ask him whether they could start doing that again, but once more, she felt she had no right.

Ultimately, Winnie decided it was best she lived somewhere else. When she told him, he asked her why, and she said she wanted a home that was hers. He insisted the cabin was hers, that he'd stop coming by if that's what she wanted. Still, she insisted, and when he asked her what she would do for work, she broke down and sobbed. So, he went to his truck and pulled out a sketchpad. He showed her a drawing of a chessboard and asked if she thought she could craft it. She examined the design, wiping her eyes so as to not blotch the ink, and answered that she could. He offered to trade its construction for her staying at the cabin for another moon, and she could find no reasons to refuse.

Winnie wasn't sure whether this sort of conflict was normal, for she had never known anyone this long in her life. The longest acquaintance she'd ever had was Farah, the outcome of which made her believe that everyone would turn against her with time.

Reed did exactly as he said he would and didn't show for weeks. At first, she figured he was giving her time to make the chessboard. By the sixth week, the pieces had all been carved, and Reed still had not shown.

Winnie began to miss him more desperately than she preferred. She thought of calling the factory and asking for him as a customer but never brought herself to do it. She found herself wandering outside multiple times a day, just staring off into the distance through white aspen trunks upon the powdered mountain, hoping for the faint roaring of an engine.

Then, one morning, when she had sunk so deep into the mattress that the springs gave out, she heard the telephone ring exactly four times.

*   *   *

They huddled beneath the ship. The cold spread throughout their bodies into an unbearable pain. They could see each other's breaths, but they couldn't read each other's minds. No one could tell who was the most afraid.

CAMELLE.
We haven't found the squid.

AUGUST.
I suppose we never did.

CAMELLE.
Most our age have found it already.
If we don't by the time we're thirty,
we may never find it at all!

SOLOMAN.
I've never felt so small.

WINNIE.
If everyone could find the squid,
it wouldn't be as desired as it is.

AUGUST.
Perhaps it's not meant for us.

SOLOMAN.
Of course. I'm nothing but dust.
I wonder if my father's found it.

CAMELLE.
I know my mother hasn't.

AUGUST.
It's not something my folks would believe.

WINNIE.
I'd never thought about it until Reed.

She looked at the floor and felt August do the same.

CAMELLE.
Well, we can't just stop trying!

WINNIE.
Some find it when they're dying.
They suddenly see it somehow.

AUGUST.
Are we dying now?

Their youth had burned to ash in a fire. Now, the ice threatened to freeze their adulthood.

As the cold reached their lungs, they wondered whether their fates were set in the sails of their sins.

SOLOMAN.
Tell the world that I was a captain.

AUGUST.
Tell my family that I loved them.

CAMELLE.
Please! Let us not talk that way!
We'll all get through this, okay?

Winnie felt a lurch inside her belly, then an uncontrollable warmth flowing out of her. A puddle spread across the floor as Camelle reached for her arm.

* * *

"Winnie, why do you pull from me?"

*"You seem to think that I'm a tree
who'd change color for those around,
yet you fail to recognize that
all my leaves have hit the ground.
I have nothing to give you!"*

"That isn't true."

"Tell me, what is it you want that I've got?
Go on! . . . That's what I thought."

"What I think is nice,
is that you're like ice.
Do you ever notice how
cold water is
so harsh on the skin,
yet so refreshing
when taken in?
You may bite at first,
but I am given life
once I absorb your words."

"Please, I'm not to be sought."

"And why not?"

"Reed, I beg you. Stay an arm's length.
Stay, or I won't have the strength . . ."

He stayed.
She ran toward him.
A kiss as wistful as a flurry of snow.

* * *

Winnie gripped the edges of her cot, the mattress
like a sheet of ice against the relentless pain burning through
her. She wanted to escape her body, to run from the flames

that threatened her insides. She couldn't tell whether it had
been minutes or days. Had she done too much, or not
enough?

The ship rumbled with every cry she gave.

WINNIE.
Camelle . . . I . . . I can't . . .

CAMELLE.
Listen. Give me your hand.
This child, coming to this land,
will be as strong as an aspen tree
because her mother is a wolf at sea.
All you need is a little trust.
Now, breathe and push!

Winnie's howl was heard from the skies. Her cot
rattled against the booming cracks of an avalanche.

CAMELLE.
Yes! You're so close!
Just a little more to go.

SOLOMAN.
I think I need to hurl . . .

Boulders of white plunged into the water as the ship
trembled violently before settling. With one last roar, a
baby's wail echoed across the ocean.

CAMELLE.
It's . . . a girl.

AUGUST.
Her hair . . . It's just like his.
Look how beautiful she is . . .

Winnie felt the fire leave her body as Camelle placed
the baby into her arms. August sat beside her on the bed, his
eyes transfixed.

WINNIE.
August, I can't tell you how sorry I am,
to get your hopes up and then—

AUGUST.
Stop. Throw that nonsense out the door.
You brought more than I could ask for.
It doesn't matter what they call the child.
It's only a word for the sake of a file.
A part of my brother is here now.
I apologize for expressing doubt.

WINNIE.
You were only looking out for yourself.
It's understood with all that wealth.
Just don't go offering things like you do.
I never wanted it from him, nor do I from you.

AUGUST.
Fine, but I'm spoiling her rotten.

SOLOMAN.
His heart, once hard, has softened.

Soloman gave Winnie a wink. Camelle dragged him away.

AUGUST.
Oh, and about my . . . attempted courting . . .
I can't believe I actually tried resorting—

WINNIE.
I still would have caught you in your lie.
Besides, you're not really my type.

AUGUST.
We were identical twins!
I look exactly like him.
Am I really that square?

WINNIE.
I have a thing for red hair.

They held back laughter behind grins. August stroked the baby's thin fiery strands.

AUGUST.
Both parents, the bravest of souls.

WINNIE.
He would have adored watching her grow.

AUGUST.
Did you love him?

WINNIE.
In my own way, I did.

* * *

Winnie wasn't sure what brought it upon Reed to ask—nearly six years after the fact—but he did.

They were in bed, reading from a novel together, when he suddenly wondered why she first came looking for a job at the factory. She had never told him about that night, or about Farah. She never thought there was a reason to. Now, as he lay there, fingers weaved with hers, she began to uncover the parts of herself that had been long buried beneath the snow.

There was a birthday party, she told him. There were no matches for the candles, so she'd gone out to buy some. The label had called to her. The trees . . . the silhouette of the house . . .

He chuckled. It was his design—a new logo created after he'd built the cabin. He was proud of it.

He let her continue.

She told him how there was an argument. She'd lit a match, must have forgotten to shake it out. She could have sworn she did, but the next thing she knew, the place was in flames. The table. . . the carpet . . . the walls . . .

As the night came back to her, she did not cry. Instead, the memory filled her with numbness, dissolving any bit of comfort she'd obtained in the last six years.

He was quiet. She told him how she had wanted to disappear after it happened, and when she'd pulled the matchbox from her pocket, it both haunted and welcomed her. In some twisted way, she'd thought being there would give her answers—answers to what happened that night, answers to who she was and who she was meant to be.

When she finished, his fingers loosened from hers. He asked her whether anyone was hurt. She didn't know.

He got out of bed, began fumbling through the kitchen drawers. She wanted to know what he was doing. He didn't answer. A moment that was supposed to be hers became one of his.

He took out a matchbox, disappearing into himself the same way he did when he was angry. When he did this, she felt lonelier than she ever did alone. It was as if she hadn't been capable of true loneliness until she'd met him.

As though he could sense her disheartenment, he looked up at her.

"This'll set you free.
Do you trust me?"

She nodded.

Reed lit a match and tossed it onto the wooden counter. It left only a faint coil of smoke.

* * *

SOLOMAN.
So . . . what shall we do next?
I think I'll go examine the deck.

CAMELLE.
Soloman, stay here. Please.
If you head up, you'll freeze!

SOLOMAN.
I'm already dead, my jewel.

AUGUST.
She's right. Don't be a fool.
You go up there, you won't come back.

Soloman gave August a smirk.

SOLOMAN.
I'm sure you'd all like that.

August furrowed his brows.

SOLOMAN.
Relax, you old grouch.
I'm just going to poke around.

He wobbled up the stairs.
Winnie looked down at the life in her arms. A panic crept over her as she realized the emptiness in her belly.
Camelle placed a hand on her shoulder.

CAMELLE.
New mothers rarely know their stuff.
You'll learn what to do soon enough.

Winnie nodded. She caressed her daughter's fingers—their touch fracturing the shell that once encased her.

WINNIE.
Camelle, the things I said . . . I was wrong.
Your ways have been right all along.
The world is good because of people like you.
Don't let those like me change what you do.

CAMELLE.
You don't know what that means to me.
You're the strongest person I know, Winnie.

AUGUST.
Let's be sure Soloman hasn't fallen into the abyss.

They heard footsteps make their way down the stairs.

SOLOMAN.
You boring lot might want to see this.

* * *

"I need to tell you something.
Will you give the phone a ring?
After your party? It's important."

"I'll return before you know it.
Now, I need to see my brother.
We always celebrate together.
He'll be thrilled with the chess set.
You've created the best gift yet."

"And what are the plans tonight?"

*"Our father got us motorbikes.
We thought we'd give 'em a crack."*

"All right. We'll talk when you get back."

* * *

Camelle followed Soloman up to the deck to find the snow had stopped. Glaciers that once stood tall and guarded were now sinking into the ocean. Ice cracked around the vessel, allowing it to break free.

The sky was indigo, filled with crystals that blurred the deeper she stared. The crystals always made Camelle feel better, no matter what was happening. Though they reminded her how small she was, they shrunk, too, the weight within her heart. She fixated on their light.

Camelle took the wheel.

Part IV:
Camelle

C amelle had a habit of starting over. Whenever she was dissatisfied with something, she would pause for a moment, take a deep breath, and begin again. For example, if she was writing a letter and made a small error, she would crumple up the entire sheet and grab a new one. If she fell off her bicycle, she would pick it up, wheel it a few yards back, and ride over the same bump in the road. She once removed all sixteen paintings from her walls to rearrange them only minutes after putting them up.

Camelle was spring. She flourished through new starts. This trait of hers carried over to the way she treated others. She forgave quite easily. Whenever someone wronged her, she would take a deep breath and pretend it never happened. Camelle believed that it was better to trust someone and have them deceive you, than to distrust someone who loved you.

She had loved Soloman since they were eight years old. Memories of the night he left had never stopped hurting her. He was the only thing she couldn't seem to start over.

* * *

CAMELLE.
Can you believe it?
We've a baby on the ship!

SOLOMAN.
Thanks to your abilities.

CAMELLE.
You should get some sleep.
We've been up for a while.

SOLOMAN.
You just delivered a child
and you're telling *me* to rest?

CAMELLE.
I haven't slept since you left.
Six long years to date
and your influence is just as great.

SOLOMAN.
It's been that long since our last meeting?

CAMELLE.
Your presence has always been fleeting.

SOLOMAN.
Do you remember what we used to say?

CAMELLE.
Of course I do. From shore to sea . . .

SOLOMAN.
And sea to shore . . .

CAMELLE & SOLOMAN.
You are mine,
and I am yours.

CAMELLE.
Mi amor.

SOLOMAN.
Mi amor.

Camelle felt the vines in her soul wither and tangle.
Tendrils turned to charcoal as buds were replaced by thorns.

CAMELLE.
We didn't know what we were saying then.
Just a couple of silly children.

SOLOMAN.
. . . Right.

CAMELLE.
Good night.
Sleep well.

SOLOMAN.
Good night, Elle.

* * *

When Camelle was eight years old, her father sat her down on the couch in the living room while her mother threw a fit in the kitchen.

"I'm no good," he had whispered to her. *"You deserve better."*

Then he'd buried his nose in the top of her head before walking out the door.

Camelle wasn't really sure what made him "no good." He had been good enough to her, and the only thing that wasn't good now was that he was gone.

As she got older, there was no doubt in anyone's mind that Camelle was an alluring woman. She was dainty and elegant, a simple delight to be around. Men seemed fond of her upon acquaintance, but eventually, they'd run from her as though her nature gave them some sort of hay fever.

They always told her the same thing her father had— that she deserved better than them, that her heart made them feel like villains. She was too good, they'd say. Too pure, and they did not want to be the one to destroy that. So, they'd leave, not understanding that they destroyed her by doing just that.

* * *

AUGUST.
Camelle's steering the ship?

SOLOMAN.
Couldn't stop her. She insisted.

She'll be fine. The ice has melted.

WINNIE.
She'd be fine regardless.

Soloman approached Winnie, who nestled a tender bundle in the crevices of her arms. At her feet, August sat on the cot holding open a book.

SOLOMAN.
How's the baby doing?
Got any names brewing?

AUGUST.
Similar to her father's, potentially.

WINNIE.
I'll think of one eventually.

Soloman squinted at the book's cover.

SOLOMAN.
Trying to find names in literature?

AUGUST.
No, no. We're just reading to her.

SOLOMAN.
. . . To that little thing?
Can she hear what you're saying?

WINNIE.
She frowns at the romantic parts.
Think she was born without a heart?
She's not very sympathetic.

SOLOMAN.
Must be genetic.
Well, I've been sent to bed.

AUGUST.
Best do what Camelle says.

SOLOMAN.
No need to tell me twice, sir.

WINNIE.
Will you tell us what you did to her?

SOLOMAN.
I ran when I should have stayed.
It was the worst mistake I've ever made.

August shut the book in his hand. He stared at it for
a moment.

AUGUST.
Soloman, the things I said before . . .

SOLOMAN.
Ah, no need to open that door.
I know you didn't mean it.

AUGUST.
Still, I wish I hadn't.

SOLOMAN.
I said some harsh things too.

WINNIE.
Should I leave the room?

AUGUST.
Funny. You should be counting sheep.
I can watch the baby while you sleep.

WINNIE.
You'll need to reach under the bed.

August bent down and pulled out a basket intricately weaved with grapevines.

SOLOMAN.
Huh. That's twice now that I've misread.
I thought you'd become our antagonist,
and instead, you've made a bassinet.

WINNIE.
Unless. . . this is all part of the plan.

SOLOMAN.
Ah! Foiled again!

August rolled his eyes as Winnie closed hers. The sound of waves lapping against the sides of the ship accompanied the breathing of mother and daughter. August and Soloman stared at the baby sleeping soundly in her basket.

SOLOMAN.
Can you believe this raisin is your kin?

AUGUST.
I can. She looks just like him.

August cleared his throat, attempting to drop the tremble from his voice.

SOLOMAN.
I'm sorry, lad. Didn't mean to upset you.
You know, I . . . I once lost someone too.
It's always the kindest souls who get taken away,
making the rest of us feel like we don't deserve to stay.

AUGUST.
That's the feeling I've struggled with exactly.
Who did you lose, if you don't mind my asking?

SOLOMAN.
My dear mother.
Although, unlike your brother,
the old man and I knew it was coming.
We just didn't have the money
to pay all those blasted bills,
and she didn't want to spend her life ill.

AUGUST.
I'm sorry, Soloman.
If I had known you then—

SOLOMAN.
No need for that, mate.

AUGUST.
Right . . . Anyway, it's getting late.
I've kept you awake long enough.
Better sleep before Camelle sees you up.

SOLOMAN.
I doubt she'd come here below the ship.
She's quite comfortable where she is.

* * *

Camelle always celebrated her birthday at the local boutiques with her mother. It was a tradition they had kept since she was four years old. They'd play a game where they would window shop for exactly one hour. If anything caught Camelle's eye, she was to keep it inside her mind.

Eventually, they'd visit the chocolate shop and pick out two pieces of chocolate to enjoy. While Camelle sat licking her fingers clean, her mother would ask her three questions.

One: "Did you see anything you like?"
Two: "Do you remember what shop it was in?"
Three: "Do you still want it now?"

If the answer was "yes" to all three, they'd go into the shop and her mother would purchase whatever it was for her, no matter the cost. One year, it was a white dress with pink bows all down the back. Another year, it was a dollhouse filled with the most delicate furniture pieces. As Camelle got older, she began to ask for things like cameras and globes. Her mother would suggest other things.

"Are you sure you don't want that silk purse?" she'd ask. "Or those glass beads?"

Eventually, Camelle would give in and pick out some embroidered gloves, which she was fond of—just not as much as she would have liked an airplane model or travel case.

* * *

CAMELLE.
You look like an uncle.

Camelle laughed as August wobbled onto the deck. The basket hung upon his arm, weighing his body down to one side.

AUGUST.
Hush. If she wakes, we're both in trouble.

CAMELLE.
Of course. I'll keep my voice low.

August gently placed the basket beside the wheel.

AUGUST.
I thought I should come say hello.
You don't appear to need assistance.

We've gone quite the distance.
There isn't a glacier in sight.

CAMELLE.
You've got that right.

AUGUST.
Where do we go from here?

CAMELLE.
I suppose wherever I steer.

AUGUST.
My folks must be having a breakdown
thinking about what I'm doing now.
I'm drifting in the middle of the ocean
instead of continuing my education,
or running our family business.

CAMELLE.
Is that what they did?
Attend university?

AUGUST.
Oh . . . no, not really.

It seemed to Camelle that elders often expected the
young to do things that they had never done themselves.
Other times, they expected only what they could understand.

CAMELLE.
Perhaps they wish they had.

AUGUST.
I don't know about that.
It's an announcement they'd like.
"My son's got a job . . . and a wife!
Forget whether he's found that damned squid!"

The baby stirred. Camelle glanced at the child, and she wondered what it was like to have a mind that had not yet developed its fears.

CAMELLE.
I'd like to think there's more to it.

* * *

Her mother had always played the piano, even in Camelle's earliest memories. It was so much a part of her that Camelle never thought about when her mother had learned it. It was only when she found the handwritten sheets of music inside the bench late one evening that she unfolded the life her mother had before her.

Camelle was usually a morning person, but there was a phase between the ages of twelve and fourteen that she had an affair with the nights. Something about the moon would bring out fragments of her imagination that the sun made her forget. In the daylight, she would only see the train across her building as a noisy nuisance. In the darkness, the empty tracks would tell stories of war and quests and heartache.

Once, it was two o'clock after midnight. The streets displayed only stillness, lit by the single streetlamp across the building. She had been woken by her blanket falling on the floor and found herself thrilled to be awake. The wool throw remained on the ground as she crept out of bed. She walked into the living room on her toes, her fingers tracing the walls.

The moonlight that peered through the balcony doors illuminated the piano, its smooth, ivory surface glistening like pearls. Her mother was always proud of the instrument's color.

"A rare find," she'd say, as houseguests nodded politely.

Camelle seldom touched the piano. It wasn't that she wasn't allowed; she just never had a reason for it. She'd give it a bit of dusting whenever she cleaned the flat, but that was the extent of it. That night was no different. She was only passing by it to go toward the balcony when she noticed the corner of a page sticking out of the bench.

That was when she lifted the cushioned lid to discover dozens of original scores, scribbled on sheets that had yellowed over time. "A Haughty Encore," "Castled Ode," "Ms Fahrenheit"—cryptic titles all dated before Camelle had been born. The handwritten musical notes skipped across straight lines, up and down, facing left, facing right. Some were in groups, some were married, and some alone. Why hadn't anything been done with them? Her mother could have been a pianist, a composer . . .

What had stopped her?

She thought to ask, but as she flipped through the ink pages—coated in blotches of devotion and torment and intensity—she feared learning the answer.

Camelle placed them back into the bench and closed the lid, gently, as to not wake her mother.

* * *

Soloman woke in his cot to find Winnie still asleep in hers. He tiptoed out and wandered into the kitchen. August was fluttering around it covered in flour like a bird that had flown indoors. The baby cooed from the basket in a corner.

SOLOMAN.
What smells so good?

AUGUST.
Pass that pan, if you would.

Soloman yawned and rubbed his eyes.

SOLOMAN.
What are we baking?

AUGUST.
Upside-down cake in the making!

SOLOMAN.
I didn't know this skill of yours.
And here I thought you were a bore.

AUGUST.
I can whip up a few cakes and pies.
I was taught by a friend of mine.

SOLOMAN.
And what's in this one?

AUGUST.
Some cherries. Bit of rum.
You'll quite like this dessert.

SOLOMAN.
I thought we were out of liquor.

AUGUST.
I hid a few bottles, give or take.

SOLOMAN.
I'm eating half this cake.

August reached into a flour sack and pulled out a
bottle. He held it out.

AUGUST.
I suppose you deserve a glass.

SOLOMAN.
Actually . . . I think I'll pass.

August placed the bottle on the counter without
pause. He handed Soloman a bowl brimming with cherries.

AUGUST.
Here, place these in lines.

Soloman pitted each one before placing it at the
bottom of the pan. When he was done, August poured the
sweet-smelling batter over them. They watched as the rubies
sank beneath the buttery waves.

SOLOMAN.
Do you think the squid is ours to find?

August slipped the pan into the oven. Then they
both sat down at the table where they had first met.

AUGUST.
I fear that giving it fervor
will only push it further.
I'm trying not to want it anymore.
I wouldn't even know what to look for.

SOLOMAN.
Some say it's the ink.

AUGUST.
And what do you think?

SOLOMAN.
I think if I don't find whatever it is,
I won't be able to bring myself to live.

AUGUST.
Why do you need it so badly?

SOLOMAN.
I'm afraid people will forget me.
As a man with no accomplishments,
perhaps I'll be recognized for finding it.
I only wish to be remembered . . . to live on.

AUGUST.
You don't need to be remembered by all.
Some who find it are never mentioned,
and there are still hunters among legends.
I'm surprised you haven't figured it out yet.
Those who matter don't forget.

SOLOMAN.
I know what you're getting at.
I fear it's more complex than that.
She and I can never be,
what with people think of me.
Only the squid can change my stature,
but it's not a painless thing to capture.
For those like me, it's not just difficult;
it requires some sort of miracle.
It's easier to hunt when you have the tools.
Respected parents . . . esteemed schools . . .
No one ever put a spear in my hands,
and I can't build one like Winnie can.
What am I supposed to catch it with?

They heard Winnie call from the other room.
August scooted his chair back and brushed the flour off
himself before Soloman placed a hand on his shoulder.

SOLOMAN.
I got this.

He stood, took the baby out of the basket, and exited
the kitchen.

* * *

When it came to Soloman, the most difficult thing
for Camelle to wrap her mind around was that she'd known
him from an early age. This was the factor that made it
impossible to see things for what they were. There was no
way for her to tell whether what they had was real or some
far-fetched romantic notion she had formed in her head.
Was she in love with Soloman, or in love with the thought of
ending up with her childhood friend? Was their long
friendship a contribution to the romantic bond she felt, or
did it merely cause a delusion? Would she still have fallen
for him if they had met later in life?

* * *

WINNIE.
I've never seen you so inspired.
Haven't your arms grown tired?

Soloman handed Winnie her child.

SOLOMAN.
Just a pull in my shoulder.
I don't mind holding her.
Having spent time with your daughter,
I don't think I'd make a terrible father.

WINNIE.
You're not all bad, I suppose.
You have a way of dissolving woes.
Sometimes I forget how to laugh,

but with you, I'm reminded of that.

SOLOMAN.
If I were being honest,
I'm absolutely exhausted.
Though I enjoy entertaining,
it can be quite draining.

WINNIE.
It's not instinctive for you to fool around?
Why do it, then . . . if it wears you out?

SOLOMAN.
I fear showing that I'm unwell,
especially around Camelle.
I don't want to be the cause of problems.
I only long to be the one to solve them.
Yet, I can't escape feeling like a burden.

WINNIE.
The love . . . You don't believe you deserve it.
I understand. I've felt the same way, too,
but you need to know there's more to you.
You bring more to our lives than just fun.

They heard a *ding!* from the kitchen.

SOLOMAN.
It appears August's cake is done.

* * *

Soloman's nature became protective when they grew into teenagers. Camelle always felt that he kept things hidden from her—the flaws of his soul and the awful things it had seen, the wounds from losing his mother that never healed. It was as though he wanted her to believe all was wonderful and everything perfect, because he could not bear for her to think otherwise. And while Camelle knew this was his way of loving her, it also pained her to know that her nature wasn't one he wanted to share things with.

When he began distancing himself from her, Camelle didn't make a fuss about it. She knew him too well. It would have only pushed him further. Instead, she watched as he went out with various girls—some she liked, some she didn't. No matter; none of them knew him like she did. Deep within the earth of her soul, she believed there were things that he reserved for her.

And then there was the fisherman's daughter.

The girl didn't attend school. She spent her days helping her father mop the decks or auction fish. She had also lost her mother, and Soloman spent some afternoons with her throughout secondary school.

Camelle knew the bond created over shared grief was something she'd never been able to give him. He hardly spoke of his mother, but when he did, she felt helpless in his pain. There was a loneliness in knowing that he shared that with someone else, though she was glad he had it. She thus decided to distance herself just as much as he had.

One day, a fellow from school invited her to the town's annual spring ball and she agreed. He was the son of a geologist, which she found fascinating. She'd had a few interactions with the boy and found him affable. Once was in the lunchroom, when they approached the line at the same time, and he let her stand in front of him. On another occasion, she turned a corner on her bicycle and nearly collided with him and his group of friends. Instead of getting angry, he'd made sure that she was all right.

Throughout each interaction with him, Camelle began to feel like someone else—someone other than the one who loved Soloman. She smiled differently, used new hand gestures, and expressed a deeper tone in her voice. Not only did she not mind her new persona—she found it quite exhilarating. Was it possible, she wondered, to be two people at once? How freeing that would be, to change out of any temperament like it were a dress.

Eventually, word got around that she and the boy were attending the ball together and Soloman approached her about it.

She was strolling home from school and had just passed a bakery when she heard the familiar voice behind her.

"I can't say I trust him."

Instantly, she was reminded of the time when they would walk home together every day. It had been years since they'd last done so.

She turned around. He stood there with his bag swung casually over his shoulder, a smudge of dirt on his nose, chewing something on the inside of his cheek.

"I didn't ask for your opinion."

She continued her way forward, losing the smell of freshly baked bread. He trailed behind her, persistent.

"I wouldn't go if I were you."

"You don't get to tell me what to do."

"Why are you angry at me?
I'm just telling you what I think.
Look, he's a bit of a sweet talker."

"Coming from you, that's not a shocker.
Takes one to recognize one, I suppose."

He grabbed her arm, his touch like a spark in a field.

"Elle, I'm asking you to be careful.
I don't want you led to slaughter."

"Why do you even bother?
We're not together, are we?
You don't need to look after me."

She pulled away from him, stomping across the cobblestones. He shouted after her.

"Oh, well, that's just unfair!
So I'm not allowed to care
unless we are to be married?
What sort of lad would I be
if courting was the only reason
that I was attentive or decent?"

Camelle hated that he was right. He was her friend, and friends looked out for one another.

She ended up not going to the ball, but she didn't tell Soloman about it either. And if he'd heard from anyone else that she'd changed her mind, he didn't mention it. Instead, they both went on as though the quarrel had never happened.

* * *

August made his way up to the deck to find a kaleidoscope of blossoms across the trees.

CAMELLE.
Look at that lovely face.

AUGUST.
I brought you some cake.

He handed her the plate before letting out a sneeze into his handkerchief.

CAMELLE.
Where did you find cherries for this?

AUGUST.
In the stockpile that Winnie hid.
I thought that they would be rotten.
The snow must've kept them frozen.

CAMELLE.
Shall I share this slice with you?

AUGUST.
Absolutely not. I've already had two.

Camelle took a bite. It felt good to have someone
indulge her for once. She had the sudden realization that she
had been very tired, and for a very long time.

CAMELLE.
I didn't know a taste this good existed!

August rubbed his nose, which was now the same
color as the dessert he offered.

AUGUST.
I must mention I had a bit of assistance.

CAMELLE.
You're lying! He offered to help?

AUGUST.
Lined the cherries all by himself.

CAMELLE.
He's full of surprises, isn't he?

AUGUST.
Speaking of. . . how have you been feeling?

Camelle put down her fork. She stared at the walls of
cake on her plate, complete with its cherry rooftop and
crumbling bricks.

CAMELLE.
I thought I had the ability to reconcile.
The truth is, I merely knew him as a child.
Is it foolish to think I know him as a man?

AUGUST.
That's assuming our natures change in a lifespan.
Whether we really change as we grow,
I'm not certain that's a fact I know.

CAMELLE.
So, you think all our traits
are usually innate?

August let out another sneeze.

AUGUST.
I'd say so, to a certain degree.
And while there are cases unique,
I believe he's still your beloved Soloman.
What things made you fall for him?

* * *

Camelle loved the building she lived in. Each apartment's balcony railing was a different color, like primrose, periwinkle, or violet. Theirs in particular was coral. Her mother would have preferred it olive, but Camelle always begged her not to have it painted.

Other than the balconies, Camelle's favorite part about the building were the vines that crawled up the eggshell walls. In spring, they were ribbons of pink and lavender. In summer, they were leafy and green and vivacious.

Every so often, the vines would grow upon the balcony railings and completely envelop the colors that made the building so charming. There was once a man who had been hired to trim them, but he disappeared for some unknown reason when Camelle was around sixteen. They never did hire someone else, so it became each resident's responsibility to trim the vines off their own railings.

Camelle made sure to keep theirs trimmed, but unfortunately, most other neighbors weren't as responsible. There were two that did so enough that you could see a peek of color on theirs, but the rest of the balconies were entirely wrapped in foliage. So, she slipped notes under all eleven doors encouraging residents to take care of it, and a few did so once or twice before the vines took over again.

This made Camelle a little sadder whenever she returned home, which she briefly mentioned to Soloman after they returned from the cinema one day. She forgot about it until the following Sunday morning, when she wandered out to enjoy breakfast on her balcony, only to look to her right to see the primrose yellow of her neighbor's railing beaming as bright as the sun. She couldn't believe her eyes, so she bent over her own railing, holding tightly so as to not topple over, and discovered the vines of all four floors had been trimmed. She thought they must have hired another man and supposed it was better late than never.

Later that day, when she was making her way down the stairwell to pick up her mother's dresses from the tailor, she ran into Mr. Derle on the second floor on his way back from the market. Seeing the old man heave bags up the stairs, she offered to help, but he lived on that floor, so she only had to carry them to his door.

As he fumbled for his keys, Mr. Derle thanked her and asked her if she could tell her friend to come earlier in the evening the next time that he needed to trim the balcony vines. Camelle didn't know what he was referring to, so he explained that the fisherman's boy had knocked on his door at about eight o'clock the night before to access the balcony, and Mr. Derle liked going to bed at nine, so it had pushed his schedule back a half an hour.

*   *   *

Camelle thought about what August said long into the evening. Though her mind was unsettled, the air remained fresh, and the trees were lush with life.

That night, she received a visit from Winnie. Camelle beamed when she saw the baby resting contentedly in her mother's arms.

CAMELLE.
Winnie! You're on your feet!

She had never seen Winnie so blissful.

WINNIE.
I wanted her to feel the sea.
Did you get to eat the cake?

CAMELLE.
More than my stomach could take.

WINNIE.
I wouldn't have been able to quit
had Soloman not devoured most of it.

The baby pursed her mouth and cooed.

CAMELLE.
Now that you're a mother,
I can't help but wonder . . .
do you feel differently?

WINNIE.
It's odd, I feel almost . . . free.
I have things I want to do.
People to see, places to get to.
I've decided to start a fund
to build a home for children.
They'd have joy I never lived,
and all the books I never did.

CAMELLE.
Do you want someone to call your own?

WINNIE.
Every so often, but I prefer being alone.
Besides . . . I don't get many suitors.
Ones who can take the cold, even fewer.
Most run from me because I know too much.

CAMELLE.
Most run from me because I don't know enough.

They burst into laughter, buds blooming through the layers of frost.

WINNIE.
Have you always wanted to be a midwife?

CAMELLE.
My mother told me throughout my life
that giving birth to me was her greatest gift.
She wants me to experience what she did,
but being a midwife is the best I could offer.
People always tell me I'd be a good mother,
as though I wasn't meant for anything else.
No one ever asks what I want for myself.

WINNIE.
And what is it that you want to be?

CAMELLE.
I bring life into a world I never get to see.
I wish I could do whatever lets me explore.
I've seen parts of the earth, but I want more.
I long to absorb as much as I can,
every drop of water, every bit of land.
It's silly, but I actually like feeling small.

WINNIE.
That isn't silly at all.
You should do what you want.

CAMELLE.
What? And quit my job?

Those women need me.
I don't have the heart to leave.
Besides, once you join the workforce,
you can't just suddenly change course.

WINNIE.
According to whose rules?

CAMELLE.
Society's! I'd be ridiculed!

WINNIE.
What are they going to do?
Get angry with you?

CAMELLE.
No, but my mother will.

WINNIE.
Consider it part of the thrill.

CAMELLE.
You have a strange definition of fun.

WINNIE.
I wouldn't know; I've never had one.
I don't know what mothers are like.

CAMELLE.
You can take mine.
Anyway, in all seriousness,
chasing a dream would be selfish.

WINNIE.
I never had the ability to dream.
You can't when you're just trying to eat.
Don't you dare throw that freedom away
if you're in a place where you can hope.
You're the most selfless person I know!
You'll find a way in whatever you choose
to not only help yourself, but others, too.

* * *

Camelle had defied her mother only once in her life.

Unlike Camelle who lived for new starts, her mother could never let anything go. Once, one of her mother's friends came over for tea and made a remark about how wonderful it was that they were able to live in such a nice flat. For days after, Camelle's mother wouldn't stop ruminating.

"She was clearly wondering how a beautician could afford all this," she said, *"implying that I have other sources . . ."*

Camelle tried to ease her. Couldn't her friend perhaps just have been making small talk with a simple comment?

"Of course not. You're foolish if you think that."

Regardless, the friend still continued coming over for tea and when she did, Camelle's mother acted like nothing had bothered her at all.

Camelle knew their money came from her father, who most likely sent it out of guilt, though she believed some part of it was love. Sometimes they'd receive small amounts weekly. Other times, they'd receive nothing for months before a large sum would end up in their mailbox in a blank envelope. She never allowed herself to think about it for more than a moment. She didn't want to imagine the things that had been done to get it. Because they never spoke of it, however, many townsfolk would make assumptions about her mother.

Another thing that Camelle's mother could never get over was the day he left. As a child, Camelle took it just as hard as she did. They would hold each other on the couch as they cried and watched the television. Later, when Camelle got to her early teens, she would have preferred to replace the date with a positive memory by going on a trip—an idea her mother rejected year after year. Camelle didn't understand what good it would do to dwell on something you couldn't do anything about, especially something that happened so long ago. If it was a death anniversary, that would be perfectly valid, but to mourn someone walking away seemed to only hurt the griever.

The night before Soloman was to part for the academy marked ten years since the day Camelle's father left. She had tried suggesting the idea of going out to the shops, but her mother had no desire to leave the flat. Instead, she spent all day alternating between rearranging the furniture and smoking on the balcony while mumbling insults at passersby. When evening came, Camelle realized they'd forgotten to go to the market, so she made poached quail eggs and toast for supper, which they ate outside. Her mother consumed three eggs and she had two. Camelle knew she would eat later with Soloman, so she didn't mind still being hungry. As she collected their plates, her mother grabbed her hand and suggested they watch television together.

"Come," she said, as she slithered into the flat. *"Come sit with me."*

Camelle followed her inside, plates in hand, as a flock of thoughts roamed through her mind. Soloman was to pick her up, and she felt guilty leaving her mother there all alone in her current state. Yet, she didn't know how long it would be until she saw Soloman again.

She told her mother that she would sit with her for a moment, but soon she'd have to spend Soloman's last night with him. To that, her mother huffed.

"Couldn't you swing by first thing in the morning?"

Camelle pondered that for a moment before deciding that was not something she wanted to do. She apologized and said no, at which point her mother shocked her by lighting a cigarette indoors, from right there on the couch.

Not knowing how to respond, Camelle turned to take their dinner plates to the kitchen. As she walked away, her mother put in the last word.

"Selfish," she mumbled while smoke filled the living room.

* * *

Petals began to fall, garnishing the sea with hues of pink. Remnants of apricot, peach, and cherry blossoms carpeted the deck, cushioning Soloman's steps one afternoon as he approached Camelle. He looked at her with hands in his pockets, curved shoulders, and pleading eyes. She tapped her fingers against the wheel and sighed.

CAMELLE.
All right. I'm ready to talk.

SOLOMAN.
I shouldn't have walked.
We can start with that fact.

CAMELLE.
We've already established that.
I want to know what happened after.

SOLOMAN.
Well, there were a few factors,
but I eventually left the academy.
Part of it had to do with money.
And I don't know . . . I . . . lost sight.

CAMELLE.
Bottle on your left, woman on your right.

SOLOMAN.
That's not what happened.

CAMELLE.
Look, captain or no captain,
neither really matters anyway.
What matters is that you didn't stay.
You didn't stay, and you didn't write.
It's as though I stopped existing that night.

SOLOMAN.
There wasn't a day I didn't think of you, Elle.

But whenever I did, I despised myself.
If I had listened and gotten you home prior,
perhaps there wouldn't have been a fire.

CAMELLE.
What? That's a ridiculous thing to say.
Going out that night was a choice I made.
You think that's the reason I'm angry?
Because you didn't get me home early?
Boy, you really are daft.

SOLOMAN.
I know it wasn't that,
but I couldn't get it out of my head.
You told me to take you home, again and again.
Thinking of that night, I can't help but hate
how I had pushed you to stay out so late.
I couldn't expect you not to hate me, too.
Besides, what did I have to offer you?

CAMELLE.
All you had to do was be there!
Anything to show that you cared.
Every fiber of my being, every piece, every line,
every part of my soul, every thought of mine
was yours. From shore to sea, and sea to shore,
I gave all of me to you. I was yours!

Drops of confusion, resentment, and longing that
she'd collected over the years at last overflowed from the
pail of her heart. She chuckled through her sobs.

CAMELLE.
Now you've lost me completely.

SOLOMAN.
Your words cut me deeply . . .

CAMELLE.
Why did you do it, Soloman? Why?

SOLOMAN.
I've told you. I'm nothing in your life.
You live in riches and harmony . . .

CAMELLE.
Who are you to speak for me?
You know nothing of my world!
I'm made of more than mere dresses and pearls.
What of my pain, my loss, my prayers?
You see a flower and forget petals have layers.

SOLOMAN.
You're right. I never saw what you went through,
nor did I ever share my battles with you.
We'd just known each other for so long,
if you'd refused my flaws, I couldn't go on.
In the end, it was easier to run than to find out.
It was spineless of me—I know that now.
I thought that if I were to leave,
you'd eventually forget me.
I never meant for you to remain hurt.

He wiped her tears with his thumb, lining the dark clouds of their memories with gold.

SOLOMAN.
I left to become someone remembered—
someone who stayed in people's minds.
And I had been in yours all this time.

CAMELLE.
How do you propose we fix this?

SOLOMAN.
I'm going to get you that squid.
I'll hunt it and give it to you.
You deserve it more than I do.

CAMELLE.
That's very kind of you to say,
but I don't want it that way.
If I'm going to have a story to tell,
I would much rather write it myself.

* * *

"Come now, you're nearly home."

"Soloman! There's smoke . . ."

"Camelle, stop! Come back here!"

"Mother's in there!"

"Miss, we can't let you through the door."

"Please! My mother's on the top floor!"

*"On the gurney, miss. Have no fear.
She's just parched. Nothing severe."*

*"Mother! I'm so sorry I wasn't home.
I shouldn't have left you alone . . ."*

"You may come along, ma'am. Just hop in."

*"Oh, thank you! Come, Soloman . . .
Sir, did you see where my friend went?"*

"I think he left, ma'am."

* * *

Camelle and Soloman were interrupted by a sneeze.
The others came up to the deck. August blew his nose into
his handkerchief, cursing all things that had bloomed during
the season. Winnie cradled her baby, who had grown several
inches since her birth.

WINNIE.
Might be time for a bit of cleaning.

AUGUST.
I wouldn't mind sweeping.

A buzz murmured across the ship. The four looked up to find an abundance of honey bees hovering from tree to tree.

SOLOMAN.
It's like a song, if one listens.

Camelle took a long, quivering breath as the chaos in her chest settled.

CAMELLE.
How can I be of assistance?

AUGUST.
You just keep on steering us,
and we'll do the clearing up.

CAMELLE.
All right. August and Winnie, you sweep the deck.
Soloman will scrub the parts that you've swept.
While that's all being done, I'll hold the baby!

SOLOMAN.
Why is the scrubbing assigned to me?

The bees' wings beat in a rapid melody as the four cleaned. They swept and scrubbed and polished until not a speck of dust floated among them. And as they tossed the fallen petals overboard and looked down at the blushing water, they almost felt clear of everything weighing them down.

* * *

After the fire, Camelle and her mother moved east of town into the modest home of her Aunt Rhea. In truth, Camelle felt relieved. Though she knew there was a possibility that her father would no longer know where they were, by the same token she was free from living off his sins.

Camelle liked her aunt very much and was appreciative she was giving them a place to stay. Despite that, her mother seemed to show resentment toward her only sister. When Camelle asked her why, her mother replied that Rhea had always been jealous of her, and that her sister was almost pleased they were in need of her now. Camelle certainly didn't sense this from her aunt, but she saw no use in arguing. Her mother never quite mentally recovered from the fire, and it was best to keep her as content as possible.

Aunt Rhea worked at the desk of the maternity ward at the town's hospital. After a few months of staying with her, Camelle's mother thought it best that Camelle accompany her aunt to work and observe things from the waiting room. Again, Camelle had no will to argue, so she took the train into town with Aunt Rhea twice a week.

On the way, they would pass the plot where Camelle's building once stood. As the train whizzed by and she glanced at the steel frames between torn-down walls, Camelle would imagine colorful balconies and sprightly vines in their place.

* * *

CAMELLE.
I realized something while standing here.

We've known each other for nearly a year.
We all had birthdays we didn't celebrate!

She stopped to stare at the horizon, wondering if she
had lived a quarter of her life or more.

WINNIE.
Unfortunately, I don't know my date.

Camelle noted the swirls and patterns across
Winnie's cheeks that marked the years she had endured.

CAMELLE.
Then we must give you one!
Let's do it now. The cleaning is done.
We'll honor all of ours, including yours.
What do you say? Party of four?

SOLOMAN.
It's not a bad plan.

AUGUST.
I suppose I can bake something again.

Winnie glanced at August. The baby whimpered.

CAMELLE.
Oh, that would be just splendid!

SOLOMAN.
I'll start setting the blankets.

August made his way through the trees with his head lowered. Winnie followed him.

AUGUST.
You can stop now, Winnie.
I know you're behind me.

He turned. Winnie pressed her nose against her child's head, absorbing the smells of vanilla and apple pie.

WINNIE.
I know your birthday's hard for you.
Thinking of it makes me miss him, too.
I could say something to Camelle.

AUGUST.
No, no. You know she means well.
Besides, moping wouldn't be his way.
Perhaps we should honor him today.

For a moment, they disappeared inside themselves—that cursed day hitting them like a windstorm—until one of them remembered what mattered.

WINNIE.
Did you like your chessboard?

August's mouth opened as he stared at the artisan before him. He chuckled at the sky.

AUGUST.
Of course.

I should have known.
Although . . .
there is an unfortunate thing.

He dug his hands into his pockets with defeat.

AUGUST.
I've lost one of the kings.

Then he went below deck, and Winnie swore his
hair looked red beneath the sunset.

Camelle saw glimpses of them through the trees. She
felt only shame as Winnie sauntered back toward the wheel.
She placed both hands over her temples and shook her head
in dismay.

CAMELLE.
I realized it the moment I saw his eyes.
It completely slipped my mind.

WINNIE.
Don't be angry at yourself.
He doesn't want to dwell.
We're still allowed fun
even if we've lost someone.
It's time we celebrate him.
So . . . what can I help with?

Camelle felt an overwhelming love for her newest
friend.

CAMELLE.
You can help August bake his dessert,
or grab Soloman a cleaner shirt . . .

SOLOMAN.
You know, I'm standing right here.

CAMELLE.
I'd do it myself, but I have to steer.

WINNIE.
I'll see what I can do.

Camelle watched Winnie walk away with the baby in her arms. There was something so natural about it; she couldn't imagine her without the child now. It was like trying to picture the earth before its soil, or a seashell before the ocean carved its shape.

She was caught off guard when Winnie turned her head back.

WINNIE.
The wheel looks good on you.

* * *

The waiting room of the maternity ward had identical wooden chairs along three walls. In the center was a table stacked with spring issues of magazines from four years prior.

Camelle would bring water to nervous first-time fathers, or play with the young children waiting to meet their new siblings. She was fond of children, especially the ones that spoke like they were adults. The need to have her own never quite found her, however. She tried hard to imagine herself with a family, but there was always a detachment—one that she worried would always be present inside her. She felt guilty about it, especially when everyone around her believed otherwise. Whenever she held a child, people always had the need to comment on it.

"A baby looks good on you," they'd tell her, eyes sparkling.

Camelle had decided to become a midwife on a regular morning at the ward. She was sitting in the waiting room, knitting little socks that she liked to give to the newborns leaving the hospital. She and Aunt Rhea had only arrived about an hour earlier when a woman with not even a handbag on her shuffled through the door. With no hesitation at all, the woman walked straight toward the waiting area and plopped down just two wooden chairs away from Camelle.

Camelle studied her at the corner of her eye. The woman didn't seem far along. Those who entered the ward were usually in labor. Most requested home visits for other kinds of appointments.

One of the nurses stopped in her tracks.

"Miss," she urged, pressing a clipboard against her chest. *"We've told you. You're only four months along. It's impossible for you to be having your baby now. You must stop coming in here."*

The woman begged. *"Couldn't you check again for me?"*

Aunt Rhea interjected from behind the desk.

"I'll watch her, Cecilia. Don't you worry."

The nurse shook her head and huffed out of the room. Camelle looked over at the woman, who breathed a sigh of relief. She put down her knitting needles, went over to the desk, and asked her aunt if she knew why the woman insisted on staying there. Aunt Rhea never looked up from the pile of papers in front of her.

"Women have their reasons," she said. *"You just have to pay attention."*

Camelle went back to her seat as she observed the woman take off her coat. That's when she noticed the bruises across her arms, the marks around her neck, the hopelessness in her eyes.

In that moment, Camelle saw an entirely different value to her aunt's work. She decided then that she was to do it too, and that was the thing that no one ever understood. It wasn't the babies that Camelle felt a need to look after—it was the mothers.

* * *

Winnie jolted awake in a cold sweat.

AUGUST.
Are you all right?

WINNIE.
Just had a bit of a fright.
Must have been dreaming.

AUGUST.
The baby's screaming.

Soloman woke and rose from his cot as Winnie comforted her daughter. The ship rocked violently.

SOLOMAN.
We should check on Camelle.

AUGUST.
Right. We're up. Might as well.

They climbed up to the deck to find dark clouds hovering over the ship.

SOLOMAN.
What the blazes has happened?

AUGUST.
The sky seems maddened!

They pushed through the rain, slipping and falling as their bodies collided with tree trunks. Camelle gripped the wheel with both hands, forcing the ship east.

CAMELLE.
All right, boys, time to help!
I hope your eyes see well.
Soloman, be sure we avoid rocks.
August, look for a place to dock.

SOLOMAN.
We've a few hurdles in sight!

AUGUST.
Keep on steering right!

CAMELLE.
The sea's pushing west!
The wheel wants to go left!
If we're going to fight the storm,
I'll need both your arms!

Soloman and August grabbed the wheel alongside Camelle. They attempted to turn it as the wind wailed and the downpour drenched them.

* * *

It wasn't that Camelle wanted to avoid him. It was more that she hadn't quite decided what to say when she saw him. She knew it wouldn't be the truth, that, she was sure of. She just had to come up with the narrative that would be best for everyone.

After a year, the guilt of having not yet visited him began to eat at her. If it had been a few months, she would have been able to blame it on a busy schedule or the move outside of town, but a year—a year made it obvious that she had intentionally not dropped by. She hoped he did not think that she didn't care for him.

Finally, on a drizzly Sunday, she forced herself through the dread and got onto the afternoon train into town. On the way, she went through different versions of what she would tell him in her head. At one point, the train sped past her old building, but she turned away from the window.

When she reached the stop, Camelle got off the train, opened her umbrella on the platform, and made her way along the docks toward the small stone cottage where Soloman's father lived.

He opened the door before she could knock. It was as though he had expected her. The rhythm of raindrops hitting her umbrella grew louder as he cleaned his hands with a rag.

"Good to see ya, darling," he said. *"Are ya hungry? I've filleted a flounder."*

Camelle shook out her umbrella as she entered. A fire was burning in the furnace. He took her coat and hung it upon a hook.

She sat at the kitchen table as he put on a kettle. He continued to prep the fish as the water boiled. She couldn't tell how much he knew, patiently waiting for him to say something that would clue her in.

He cut a lemon into thin, round slices.

"I told him to write ya," he said finally.

He grabbed a stick of butter from the fridge. Camelle watched as he compiled everything into a baking dish, laying the lemon slices across the flounder and sprinkling it all with parsley. He slipped the dish into the oven. The kettle whistled.

He brought her tea in an old, chipped mug that had been there since she was a child. Its familiarity eased her. She warmed her hands on it as he sat down across from her with his own stained cup.

"I don't expect ya to forgive him," he told her.

Camelle was surprised that he knew. That meant Soloman had shared what he did. There was no version of the story to tell now. The truth had already introduced itself.

She spoke as she stared at the steam rising from her mug.

> *"I'm so sorry I haven't come by.*
> *I honestly don't know why—"*

He put up his hand.
"Ya need to stop doing that."
She looked up at him, puzzled.
"This didn't happen to me," he said. *"It happened to you."*

He pushed his cup to the side and put his elbow on the table.

"Look, forget my blasted son. And forget ya mother, too. What are ya doing for yourself?"

Camelle told him she'd been training to become a midwife. As she expanded on the details of her program, Soloman's father remained unmoving. She grew nervous as he studied her face. Somehow, she knew he could read the inflections of her voice. The more she told him, the more foolish she felt. When she finally finished, he leaned back in his chair.

"You haven't found it, darling," he said after a moment. *"Eventually, you'll have to venture into the waters."*

She was surprised at how blunt he was about the squid. No one had ever spoken of it to her before.

Camelle assured him that it was on her mind. Now that they no longer received money from her father, she needed to make sure her mother was taken care of. Perhaps finding the squid would show her mother a new way of living—one where they could exist beyond bitterness and grief. Discovering it would allow Camelle to share the knowledge and help those around her.

> *"I'm going to find it, and when I do,*
> *I'll show others how to find it, too."*

He gave her a smile. It reminded her of Soloman's in the way that it knew something she did not, both caring yet condescending.

"Yer just like his mother," he said.

She looked him in the eyes, letting herself absorb the pain within them. He continued.

"If you're hunting it for others, you'll never find it."

She opened her mouth to argue but feared that he was right. Instead, she sipped at her tea. The heat got her tongue, then her throat. She tried to start over, to shake off the feeling that bubbled in her chest, but alas, she could not.

The timer on the stove dinged.

* * *

Below deck, Winnie sat upon her bed, clutching her baby against her chest. As the ship rocked, the cots began to slide about the room. She grabbed a blanket and wrapped it around herself, tightening it around her child to hold her in place. Her cot slammed against a wall, taking them with it. She leapt off and ran toward the stairs.

Both rain and ocean water splashed at her as she reached the deck. She pulled the blanket over her daughter's head and forced herself between the trees, trudging toward the wheel. Through the spray of the sea, she could see the others holding on with all their might.

WINNIE.
Is anyone harmed?

CAMELLE.
No, but we need your arm!

Winnie looked down at the baby crying against her chest. She kissed her daughter's head and positioned herself beside the others.
Eight hands on the wheel.

CAMELLE.
All right, friends, keep it steady!

Lightning struck the sea. The four looked at one another.

CAMELLE.
Ready?

Their arms twisted around each other as they fought against the wheel. They could see the moon behind enraged clouds, its beams like strings pulling at the ocean.

CAMELLE.
Point toward the waves as they get closer!
Face them head-on or they'll knock us over!

High swells curled and kissed the heavens as the ship rose and fell with them. The water showed no mercy, swallowing them again and again as they held on with all their courage. They felt as though they would never know stability—that they would be trapped in restlessness and turmoil forever. It was only when their fingers burned that the ship began to steady.

CAMELLE.
That's it! Keep hanging on!
It'll be darkest before the dawn.

Black ink seeped into the sea.

The gloom from above spilled into the water. The rumbling settled as cerulean poured across the canvas of the sky. The clouds acted like they had never rained.

Then the horizon came into view, revealing something straight ahead.

SOLOMAN.
Is that an island afloat?

AUGUST.
That's no island. We're back home.

The four realized that they had boarded a ship and endured many long months on board just to return from whence they came. As the vessel inched forward, they found buildings where trees once stood and docks where water once flowed. The land was noisy with the sounds of others, the air filled with ambition and promise.

WINNIE.
You could hardly recognize it.

CAMELLE.
The possibilities feel . . . endless!

SOLOMAN.
How did they build new things in a blink of an eye?

AUGUST.
Are they new? Or did we miss them the first time?

Among the noise of automobiles and heels clicking upon pavement, they took notice of the way the water glistened from the sun and how the wind swirled the leaves off the ground. They heard the chirping of birds over voices and smelled the soil over smog. They searched for tranquility within the bustle and found it remained.

The anchor dropped, and a sea of faces appeared around them—faces that had been aboard the same ship all along. Students overwhelmed by the paths they were to choose for themselves. Young workers doubting the paths they'd chosen. Newlyweds wondering if they were in for better or worse. Their voices murmured as they disembarked—some defeated that they had not found the squid, others still determined yet.

And as the four gazed at the crowd around them, they recognized that they were not alone. They looked at each other with wonder as the clamor of other minds filled what was once a lonely silence. Fellow passengers brushed by them, catching their cold and heat, feeling their flutter and calm.

They released the wheel and walked beside other bodies, stepping their feet upon familiar earth, and moving from the wavering deck to solid ground. Their eyes met, hearts beating in harmony. One by one, they gave each other parting words.

CAMELLE.
Oh, August, how I'll miss you so.

AUGUST.
You're stronger than you know.
You keep him in check now.
Don't let him bring you down.

CAMELLE.
I would never.

AUGUST.
Friends forever?

CAMELLE.
Only if you're fun.

AUGUST.
Right. Good one.

They held onto each other, their embrace both gentle and vibrant. Behind them, Soloman made faces at the baby.

SOLOMAN.
I'll miss you, little raisin.

WINNIE.
Be sure to visit, Soloman.

Soloman looked into Winnie's eyes, green sprouting through snow.

SOLOMAN.
You're a great being, I hope you're aware.
I wish nothing but luck for you out there.

WINNIE.
I thought you'd know me after all this time.
Who needs luck when you're as able as I?

SOLOMAN.
Ah, I confuse you with someone else.

WINNIE.
I admit, I'll miss your nonsensical self.

SOLOMAN.
If you ever need a break, I'll befriend you.

WINNIE.
And if you ever need a friend, I'll defend you.

They shook hands—his, coarse and cool; hers, soft and warm.

Winnie turned to Camelle, who immediately was stricken by a flood of tears.

WINNIE.
Don't you dare be that way!
I refuse to cry today.

CAMELLE.
I'm trying not to, I swear.

They laughed as Camelle wiped her eyes.

WINNIE.
I hope you know that I care.
You brought me my little redhead.

Camelle stroked the baby's thin, fiery strands.

CAMELLE.
I do. And I've decided on what you said.

WINNIE.
What will you do if you're not a midwife?

CAMELLE.
I've got something in mind.
They'll doubt I can do it as a woman,
but there's no reason why I couldn't.

WINNIE.
If anyone gives you trouble, come find me.

CAMELLE.
I will. I love you, Winnie.

Before Winnie could find the words, arms flung around her. A little way from them, August nudged Soloman.

AUGUST.
Are you done feeling sorry for yourself?
What do you plan to do about Camelle?

SOLOMAN.
She should be with someone less disturbed.

AUGUST.
It's not too late to be the man she deserves.
Question is, are you willing to become him?

Soloman looked to Camelle. Golden rays ignited around her as she made her way down the dock. He began after her.

AUGUST.
Soloman?

Soloman spun around.

AUGUST.
The people we lost . . . Reed . . . Your mother . . .
We're worthy of life just as much as they were.

Behind Soloman, the sun's glow went from yellow to orange. He gave a nod.
Then he ran.

Winnie approached August and stood beside him. They watched Soloman glide down the dock after Camelle.

AUGUST.
She's trying to walk slow, isn't she?

WINNIE.
Oh, absolutely.

August pulled out an envelope.

AUGUST.
Here. Take this letter to my family.
Tell them everything you told me.

WINNIE.
What if I'm not what they want?

AUGUST.
Don't have those thoughts.
You're bringing a part of him.
You'll be a daughter to them.
They'll adore you, I promise.
Just be sure to give them this.

He handed Winnie the letter.

WINNIE.
It smells like mint leaves.

AUGUST.
Right. Same pocket. Sorry.

WINNIE.
Where will you go?

AUGUST.
For now, somewhere alone.

Winnie reached into her own pocket and pressed a key into his palm.

WINNIE.
Follow the dirt road up the mountain.
When the road narrows, you've found it.
The cabin will soon come into view.

AUGUST.
Thank you.

Winnie noticed something blue in his smile.

WINNIE.
Live free, now that you can.

AUGUST.
I'm devising a new business plan.
Reading to her put the idea in my mind.
It's the perfect trade, I'm sure you'll find.
Did you know paper is made from aspen trees?

WINNIE.
And books need paper. That is interesting.

AUGUST.
Quite. I intend to see this through.
Take care of my niece, will you?

WINNIE.
We'll be at the manor, waiting.

She pulled a chess piece from her pocket. It was painted red.

WINNIE.
I made you another king.

August held it in his hand, stroking the carvings with his thumb.

AUGUST.
I love it. I'll never lose it again.
I'll be sure to place the queen next to him.

WINNIE
What will happen to your family name?

The baby cooed.

AUGUST.
She'll make it known in other ways.
Don't you worry. It'll be good.

WINNIE.
See you then, Norwood.

August glanced at the two identical scars across his arm. He decided that he would first live in isolation. Just for a while, so he could silence other voices to allow his own to grow louder. He needed his voice loud enough so that when he returned to the world, he would hear it no matter what noise came his way. Perhaps then, he would taste happiness.

Meanwhile, Winnie began the journey toward her new family. Her stomach fluttered as she thought of going from a life of solitude to a bustling household. She held her daughter close. The vines within her soul began to unravel, delicate buds blooming upon them.

Soloman chased Camelle to the end of the dock. He stepped in front of her, catching his breath as she held hers.

SOLOMAN.
I'll be beside you for as long as you let me stay.
Live with me in a house made of cake?

CAMELLE.
And who will pay for it?

SOLOMAN.
August.

CAMELLE.
Funny.

SOLOMAN.
Forget money.
You're everything, Elle.

CAMELLE.
That's all fine and well,
but it's my turn to disappear.

I've decided not to stay here.

SOLOMAN.
Where will you go, then?

CAMELLE.
To become a captain.

SOLOMAN.
Captain Camelle. I must admit,
it does have a nice ring to it.

CAMELLE.
First, I'll attend the academy.

SOLOMAN.
Right here is where you'll find me.

CAMELLE.
Then I'm going to see the world.

SOLOMAN.
I'll look forward to your return.

CAMELLE.
I'll be gone a long time.

SOLOMAN.
I'll be sure to write.

Camelle thought for a moment.

CAMELLE.
No more drinks.

SOLOMAN.
Down the sink.

Camelle scoffed.

CAMELLE.
Did you fall from the sky, mi amor?

SOLOMAN.
No, my love. I washed ashore.

Soloman hopped onto a passing trolleybus. He clung onto the door frame with one hand, hanging out of it as the driver shouted at him. He gave a wink to Camelle, who shook her head at the ruckus.

It was time Soloman saw his father. Family was the most important thing there was. He would be proud to become a fisherman like him. The thought gave him a sense of pride he did not expect. He would become a fisherman, and someday he'd board the ship she chose to sail.

As Camelle watched him disappear into the crowd, it no longer mattered to her what would become of them. Life was merely brief encounters with the sun. She felt a bliss from what she had accomplished. In a world of takers, she had succeeded to only give. This realization gave her a sense of self-worth she never had before, and as the bus shrunk into a blur, something else became very clear. While most found their strength by changing, she had found hers by remaining who she was.

     Our story ends at the edge of the sea, where the sky is painted orange and blue, pink and yellow. It is neither then, nor now. There is no time to lose, yet much to gain. Days are marked only by the strength of the moon.

     There are four present. How or when they got there, we may never know. What we do know is that they found one thing through four very different means.

     And so they head in four different directions, for what had brought them together now brought them to part.

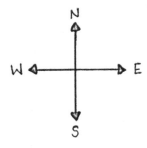

Epilogue

"Norwood House Books may provide the best,
but paperbacks must only cost sixpence.
No one should be deprived of our reads
because they don't have the means.
Is that all understood?"

"Yes, Miss Norwood."

"Rieka, there you are!"

"Mother, I didn't go very far."

"I've looked for you all over the estate.
The flowers have arrived at the gate.
Today's no time for business."

"You know I can't help it.
How do the children like the books?"

"They haven't had time for a look.
They're practicing their singing

before the bells start ringing.
Your Uncle Leo has gone insane.
He's attempting a house-sized cake!"

"This wedding is special, Mother.
Besides, Soloman's like their brother.
They only want the finest for him."

"Well 'the finest' is destroying our kitchen."

"I assume the captain's written her vows."

"She's finished it just now.
I even suggested a line:
'It's about time!' "

"Ah, but we know what really occurred.
It was he who waited for her."

"Right. Oh, we've only got an hour!
Come, now. Let's get the flowers."

"And what will the weather be?"

"That . . . we'll have to see."